… Standing at the edge of a cliff, Terrin stared down on green trees that faded into the distance, so thick that you could hardly tell they were leaves and not grass. From up here, it didn't look too spooky, but she knew this was the very edge of the Dark Forest.

To her right, the river rushed over the cliff and crashed down into a small clearing, but the sound seemed dull, muffled by a steady, buzzing hum. Below, a stream from the waterfall's base flowed away into the trees.

Beside it lay a black body, cruelly twisted.

She was locked to the spot not by fascination with the body, but by the strange prickling sensation along her back. She had felt that cold tingle before.

Magic.

Four spirits moved out from the trees, pale figures gliding towards the carcass. They formed a half circle around it. Then they looked up at her.

Even from this distance, she could tell they were smiling.

Terrin put her arm out, trying to reach something to steady herself against, but found nothing.

She couldn't tear her eyes away, and though there were no words in the strange humming, she knew they were calling to her. They were pulling her forward, closer to the edge.

She felt her body sway forward.

Her mind screamed …

HUNTED

THE RIDDLED STONE
BOOK TWO

TERESA GASKINS

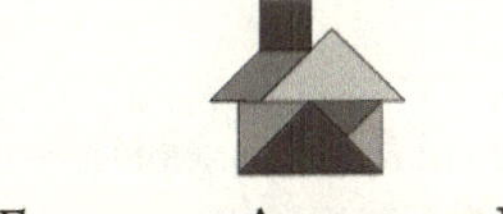

TABLETOP ACADEMY PRESS

PART ONE

൛ 1 ൛

Terrin

Terrin crashed through the bushes, thorns scratching at her arms and legs. She stumbled forward as her foot dropped farther than she expected.

She caught herself against the ground with her hands, pulling herself forward. Though she was only eight years old, growing up in the forest had made her agile. She was up and running again in a second, barely breaking her stride.

Underfoot, twigs and leaves crackled. Behind her she could hear a *thump, thump, thump* and the snapping and scratching of twigs against scales as something large leaped through the underbrush.

Wraiths were normally shy creatures. Why was this one so aggressive?

She ignored the cramp that stabbed at her, the sweat stinging her eyes, and the pain in her chest as she gasped for air, struggling to pick her feet up higher and clear the plants that reached to tangle her ankles.

She burst into an unfamiliar clearing and paused, looking around. The ground dropped away in front of her, how far down she couldn't see. She was surrounded by woods except for a gap between the trees and the cliff. A river to her right fell off into a waterfall, but Terrin could barely hear it over her own pounding heart.

She turned away from the stream, forcing her weary legs to move. But she was too slow, and before she had taken a step, a great weight slammed into her. She let out a cry as she fell forward to the ground.

Something warm touched the back of her neck.

"Help, help, someone help me," she yelled.

But the forest people never wandered this close to the Dark Forest. Here the woods were cold and unwelcoming.

There would be no one to help her.

The pressure on her back eased enough for her to roll and face the beast. All she could see was its flat, black head and those huge golden eyes with slit pupils, watching her. Its mouth lolled open, pink against the dark skin, and the white teeth dripped with dark gray saliva.

She heard its scaly skin ripple as it crouched closer to her. Its tongue ran over its teeth, and its nostrils flared so wide that Terrin could have almost fit her hand in them.

Then the beast turned its gaze to the left and growled, its nostrils narrowing to slits.

It spun and leaped away, its long, thick tail swinging only inches above her head. The tail disappeared from above her, and she sat up enough to watch as it cleared several bushes. Despite the scales and the lizard-like head and tail, the creature moved more like a huge cat. She supposed its ability to blend with the shadows had earned it the name wraith.

She hoped her father was okay. He had been teaching her to track when they sighted the wraith and stopped to watch it for a while. Even though they lived in the forest, wraiths were rare and usually avoided people.

Then the beast had spotted them and attacked.

Her father had ordered her to run, and she'd obeyed too quickly to see what he had done. But surely he was all right, surely he'd come and find her, and perhaps he would know why the wraith had acted strangely.

Exhausted by the breakneck run and fear, Terrin felt herself fading into darkness. She struggled weakly to stay awake.

Through the fog of weariness, she noticed the silence.

That was odd.

The forest glimmered with a reddish shade that meant the sun was setting, but where were the cheerful chirps of birds and the rustle of grass as creatures ran to and from their dens? There was nothing, as if some sort of void had sucked away all the life of the forest.

Not even the buzz of bugs stirring about.

And she could barely feel the breeze against her skin.

A tingle ran up her spine, but at the same time it was as if the tingle was floating off to her left.

It was… magic?

Groaning, Terrin pushed herself to a sitting position. She froze as she met the eyes of a pale, rose-colored ethereal being, floating an inch off the ground at the edge of the clearing. As she stared into its blank eyes, a strange humming started.

The thing approached with gliding strides, just short of the grace of floating, and the tingling sensation grew stronger, like hundreds of pinpricks in her back.

Terrin fought back tears of fear. She was a forest girl, and she refused to cry.

The being stretched out a hand toward her, and the humming rose in pitch as the thing's fingers brushed against her cheek. The tingling turned into a chill. Her body locked up. Her instincts told her to run, or defend herself, but she could only tremble.

She realized that this must be a spirit. Raw magic, without need of a magician to uphold it.

Some said that spirits were the souls of strong magicians who had been especially close to nature. But Terrin knew now they couldn't be—there was nothing human about this creature. Those empty eyes confirmed what the freezing sensation already told her.

Spirits were evil.

Terrin cried out for help again, positive that the ethereal monster would devour her soul.

An answering call came from the forest, "Terrin, Terrin?"

She recognized her father's voice and screamed her reply. "Father! Father, quickly."

The spirit withdrew its hand and turned its shimmering head towards the sound of twigs and leaves snapping under foot. Her father crashed into the clearing, panting. The spirit took a step back, then turned and rushed into the woods. Terrin was sure that the thing really was floating this time.

She scrambled to her feet and grabbed her father's hand. He pulled her close, his hug chasing away the chill.

"F-Father, did you see it? It tried to eat me."

"I saw the wraith. It's gone now. You don't need to worry about it anymore."

"No, Father, the spirit. Did you see the spirit?"

Tears pounded at the back of her eyes, but she held them back with slow, trembling breaths.

"No, honey, I didn't see the spirit." He frowned and knelt to her level. "Was there one?"

"Yes. It was horrid."

"It doesn't matter. You'll be fine now, my girl. Come on, let's go home. We're late and your mother will be worried," he said. But he was still frowning as he hugged her again, his hand running through her tangled hair.

She leaned against her father as they walked, still sore from her run earlier. But she was of the forest tribe of Xell, and she would not show weakness. Not until she was home, anyway.

Terrin glanced at her hands. They still had dried blood on them, from her fall, but there was no sting. Frowning, she gave them a closer examination.

The scrapes had already healed.

ᴄꙮ 2 ᴄꙮ

Terrin, 10 years later

"So, lad, I reckon yer headed to the capital to volunteer for th' army?"

The villager's deep voice carried up the hall from the inn's common room. Terrin paused by the doorway, listening.

"And how do you reckon that?"

Terrin recognized Arnold's voice and almost laughed when she realized who the farmer was talking to. Despite his boyish looks, Arnold was already a knight.

Though his knighthood would surely be revoked, if they were ever caught. The terms of Chris's banishment would apply to anyone who dared to help him. And they had been traveling with Chris, until the idiot decided to run off on his own in a misguided attempt to keep them safe.

Now they had to hunt him down, and the rain that had been falling on and off—mostly on—for the past two days didn't help.

The villager spoke again. "Bah. If yer not headed there now, ya will be soon enough. Soon as the war starts, and we all know that won't be long. Personally I think the king's doing a botched job of it. We all knew another war would be coming any time now, but did he start preparing? No! He waits to th' last minute."

"My poor Nessa," moaned another voice. "She won't be able t' handle it. All alone like. She's been doing alright since her mother died, but I don't think she could take it if I was called away now."

"Stop yer groaning, Clark. Nessa's stronger 'an a pair of ox. She's as likely t' be called as ya."

"Now that's cruel!"

Arnold broke in. "Tell me, what exactly have you heard about this upcoming war?"

The second farmer, Clark, answered. "Some caravan got burnt up real good. Heard the Crown Prince found it 'imself. They say there's proof a South Raecan lot were the ones attacked it."

The first farmer gave a snort. "We coulda attacked years ago, got ahead of 'em. Now we've let them have the first move! It'll take months t' amass a frightful force t' oppose 'em. As I say, the king shoulda been preparing!"

"Wait," Arnold said. "Are you saying the king shouldn't have had hope for a lasting peace? Building up an army would have brought war for sure."

"War's coming, boy. Been doin' so fer a long time. Peace'll ne'er last," said the first farmer.

"Aye. Not till the king's got 'em under his belt," added Clark. "And th' longer he takes, th' more we simple farmers suffer for it."

"You forget," said Arnold, "the nobles always have knights in training. And the king has allies he can call upon, if there is a war."

"Sure, the knights'll come. But th' allies won't. Only ones close 'nough are the Yorcs." A couple farmers gave low laughs at this. "And th' Isles. No help from either o' them."

Terrin's sharp ears picked up someone muttering, "Th' Yorcs

need t' be taught a lesson much as th' South'ners," under his breath.

Her mouth pulled back into a deep frown.

"Well, as ya can see, we don' have no allies close 'nough to help. 'At leaves th' lords and their knights."

"And," finished Clark, "th' lords and knights can't fight no war on their own. So they'll be sendin' fer us farmer folk. You'll see."

Terrin almost smiled as she imagined Arnold's flustered face—being lectured about the ways of war when he'd been taught by real knights. But she was too annoyed by the comment about the Yorcs.

At least Nora was still in their room and had not heard.

☙

Christopher

Chris pulled his cloak tighter and shivered, poking his pitiful attempt at a fire with his foot.

The heavy drizzle plastered his hair flat. He tried to tuck one loose strand behind his ear, but it stuck to his forehead. The black mess was growing long enough to get in his eyes, and he feared the day he would have to comb it.

Beyond the fire, he could see Thomas curled in his blanket. The older man had fallen asleep quicker than Chris would have thought possible in this constant rain.

He himself could not sleep, but it was more than just the rain. How was he supposed to make plans when he had no idea where they were headed? His last dream had shown him five people riding into the early morning sun. So he and Thomas were travel-ing east—though the sun had yet to show its face.

He had told Thomas of the dream, but he hadn't mentioned the extra three people. No reason to worry him. Still, Arnold,

Terrin, and Nora had been constantly on Chris's mind since then. He was sure he'd done the right thing when he left them. His presence had brought them nothing but danger.

He sneezed.

Of course, he was also endangering Thomas, but the older man knew what he was doing. The others had followed him on blind faith. They'd expected him to head to Diamond Isles and live a peaceful life in exile. Instead he had dragged them into a quest to follow magic riddles that sounded like nonsense.

A quest to what?

The cave where King Miles found the Riddled Stone and its five Shards, long ages ago? If he got that far.

And if he did, what good would that do him?

The harpies had shown him the first riddle—the same one that launched King Miles on his quest during the Great Raecan War—carved in ancient runes deep in their secret cave. The message had warned that "until the hidden are retrieved, you cannot be free."

Was he being foolish to hope that he could find the missing Shard, which he was accused of stealing, the reason he had been banished? But whoever had taken the Shard had disappeared without leaving a clue—not one that didn't point to Chris, anyway.

How could an old cave, even a mysterious, magical cave, have any proof of his innocence?

No, now wasn't the time to worry about that. He would deal with that when he got there. If that was where the magic was leading him.

For now, he just had to worry about what to do next. He let his mind wander over the maps he'd studied in school. The challenge would be not to get lost in the forest. Probably their best bet was to swing north and find the cliff that marked the southern edge of the Dark Forest. That would make it easier to keep from getting turned around, and they should be able to pass quickly and unnoticed.

Yes, this was best. He would deal with things as he got to them. Thinking too far into the future or past would only dishearten him.

At this point, he couldn't give up, or he'd have nothing.

$\mathcal{O}$ 3 $\mathcal{O}$

Arnold

The sun glimmered down, reflecting off the smooth mountain stone and blinding anyone who looked the wrong way. The three companions rode slowly down the switchback road, Arnold's eyes pinned on the back of Terrin's head to avoid the shining mountain peaks. Nora followed behind.

Terrin had insisted they leave the inn just after breakfast—she'd almost refused them that—to cross the ridge and head out of the mountains. They would easily reach the forest of Xell before evening.

But in Xell, finding Chris would be like finding a toothpick in a wood pile. If he was even there.

They had tracked him as far as that last riddle cave. Arnold wondered, had Chris been able to read the ancient markings on the stone? It had looked like a jumbled mess—but the first stone had been covered with strange marks, too, and somehow he had understood them.

That first message had warned of danger and death, and the

harpy seer Andrea had hinted at something terrible about to happen. Then this morning they heard rumors of war brewing in the south. Was that what the riddles were about?

How would they ever figure it out, if they couldn't find Chris?

Outside the riddle cave, they had found clear tracks headed down the mountain to the east. He couldn't have been too far ahead of them. But the sun set before they could catch him, and then the rain had come and nearly washed the whole trail away. Without Nora's mountaineering skills they would have been stuck until the path dried out.

But the tracks were gone. Arnold had no idea how they would find Chris now, and the longer they rode the less hope he had.

Terrin had decided that Chris was headed out of the mountains into the forest, and this was the quickest path down—practically the only path that wasn't washed out. Arnold suspected she was being influenced by the desire to go home.

Few of the forest folk traveled as far as Fredricburg, where the four of them had met and become friends, even though the school was known as the best in North Raec. Terrin had never been at home in the city or in the surrounding plains. She had seemed more comfortable in the small woods north of town, where they had explored as children in their free time, but even then she'd been wary. So Arnold couldn't help but wonder how different she would be in the forest of Xell, where she had been raised.

He supposed her outward stubborn streak would remain, but he wondered if she might lose some of the angry cheek she had given even the headmaster. After all, she had repeatedly boasted that forest children were taught to respect their elders.

But Arnold knew that her outward confidence and ferocity were just shields. She was as vulnerable to doubt and fear as himself—sometimes more so. He knew her mind was constantly replaying her behaver towards Chris, wishing she hadn't been so harsh.

He would never forget that time when he had seen her—

"Wolves!"

Terrin's voice startled Arnold out of his reverie. Instinctively he started to pull back on Rich's reins as Terrin pulled to a stop in front of him, but when he realized what she'd said, he nudged the horse forward to stand beside Terrin. Before them on the path stood three large wolves. Behind him, Nora pulled her own horse to a halt.

The wolves were obviously tired. One had its left eye swollen tightly shut, with fresh claw marks over it. All bore several such claw marks in various places and were missing clumps of fur. Some of the scratches still bled.

Arnold hissed through his teeth. "We need to back away slowly."

"I know," said Terrin, a bit too sharply.

The largest of the wolves growled.

Arnold glanced back to Nora. She was slowly moving Minty back. The horse's nostrils flared, and her ears flickered. Nora leaned forward, patting her neck and shushing her.

Terrin was examining their surroundings. A couple yards to their right a rocky wall stood head-high beside the path, while on their left the steep slope of stones and scraggy mountain grasses offered no place to hide. As she slowly turned forward again Arnold caught her eyes for a second. He saw the flashes of anger behind her glowering eyes. She gathered her reins and signaled Leaf to back. The horse took two quick steps and tossed its head, snorting.

The third wolf moved past the leader and then crouched low, snarling. Its fur was tinged ginger-red, but Arnold couldn't tell if the color was natural or if it was blood.

Taking his reins in his left hand, he signaled Rich to move in front of Terrin. His right hand moved almost unbearably slow to loosen his sword.

The three wolves began to spread out. One-eye's flattened ears almost blended with his head. And his eye seemed to flicker from Arnold to the lead wolf. On the other hand, the ginger's eyes were locked on Arnold, and its snarl sent a shiver down his back.

"I don't think this is working," whispered Arnold.

He glanced back at Terrin, who was slowly reaching for her bow. If there was a fight, it would start before she had a chance to string it.

And as the lead wolf began to move forward, adding his own snarls to the ginger's, it was looking more and more like a fight. He signaled Rich to back with short steps, keeping him between the wolves and the girls. But the leader moved forward with matching steps. Arnold loosely wrapped his reins around his saddle's pommel and slowly reached back for his shield.

Too slowly. The ginger lunged.

Arnold signaled and Rich pulled into a rear, then pivoted. The wolf landed to their right, and as Rich fell back to all fours Arnold swung his sword down.

The blade caught the red wolf's shoulder and it sprang back with a yelp. The other two quickly charged in. Arnold turned his horse again and his sword flashed in the air between him and the closest wolf—the leader—which pulled back as if stung. Arnold pivoted Rich, and the horse pranced toward One-eye.

One-eye retreated with bared fangs, a growl rumbled in its chest. Then it lunged forward, forcing Rich back to avoid its angry jaws. Both the lead wolf and the ginger joined in, pushing the horse back with their snapping teeth.

"Arnold, the edge!" Nora called.

Arnold instinctively glanced at them. Terrin had dismounted and strung her bow.

Rich slipped. For a second Arnold felt the horse begin to slide down the stony slope, then Rich lunged forward onto the path.

The wolves scattered.

Arnold didn't wait for Rich to fully steady himself before turning the horse to rush One-eye, the nearest wolf. It started to pull away, now wary of the horse, but Arnold's sword caught it behind the ears.

The wolf collapsed, and he pulled his sword free. He turned to face the leader, just as an arrow struck it down.

He swung his head, searching for the ginger wolf, but it came to him. The reddish-gray blur registered in Arnold's peripheral vision, and he started to pull Rich around to face it. Then pain shot up his left arm as the lunging wolf's teeth sank into his wrist. The unexpected power of the wolf's momentum carried him off his horse, giving him barely time to kick his feet free.

He landed on his sword arm, the impact knocking his breath away and causing him to release his sword. He rolled and slid for several feet, ending face down in a patch of dew-soaked grass. The wolf was carried over him, nearly pulling his arm out of joint, but it released his wrist as it passed. It hit the ground and tumbled over, sliding into the mountain wall.

The beast lay still, stunned and maybe even dead. Arnold shut his eyes for a second, pulling a deep breath. Then he opened them, and the ginger was dragging itself to its feet. Snarling more than ever, it staggered towards him.

⁎

Nora

Before the wolf could reach Arnold, Rich spun with stunning speed. His back hooves kicked out, striking the ginger straight on, and sending it flying back into the wall with a crack that made Nora's stomach twist. At the same time, she heard a sharp twang. An arrow smacked into the wolf's chest, no doubt killing it—if it wasn't dead before.

For a moment Nora could only stare at the scene before her. The air seemed eerily silent after the bow shot. Then something clicked in her mind, and she swung off Minty and ripped her bag free from her horse's back. With a quick movement she twisted the reins around the saddle horn before she turned toward Arnold.

She forced herself to walk and to take several deep breaths. Rich turned to face her, his eyes and nostrils wide.

"Whoa, good boy," she said, gently patting the horse's forehead before she crouched next to Arnold. The horse was well trained, and now that the danger was gone, he held perfectly still.

"Is he okay?" asked Terrin, kneeling beside Nora.

"I'm fine, and I'm right here," said Arnold as he rolled to his back and started to prop himself up. But when he put weight on his left hand, he collapsed again with a yelp.

"Stop getting dirt all over it," Nora said.

She grabbed his forearm and turned the wrist over. Thin, gray mud smeared over the wound, mixed with the red of fresh blood. As she held his hand, he pushed himself into a sitting position.

"Of course it had to catch you on your wrist," Nora muttered. Then, louder: "Terrin, get me my water skin. I need to see the wound."

Terrin leaped into action, but instead of turning to Minty, she quickly detached Arnold's skin from where it hung over his saddle-horn.

As she handed it to Nora, she asked, "Is it bad?"

Nora splashed the water across his wrist, causing Arnold to groan through clenched teeth. The dirt washed away, exposing the torn flesh for a second. Then blood welled up, hiding it again.

Flowing blood was good—it would cleanse the wound. But not enough.

"We need to move," she said. "We have to find a stream."

She stepped back to let Arnold scramble to his feet. Then turning to Terrin, she added, "An animal bite is always bad."

$\wp$ 4 $\wp$

Trillory

Stretching out her arms, Trillory whirled herself in a circle. She loved the freedom of being alone in the north wing's small common room. The bustling manor of Duke Grith seemed almost empty, now that the king had summoned the duke to a council in Coricstead. Many of the nobles and noble-wannabe courtiers had already scattered, returning to their own homes to prepare for the expected war.

She stopped spinning and let her arms drop. Her father, Earl Fredrico, had always said the rivalry with South Raec was long past, that they were friends now. Others strongly disagreed.

Would there really be a war?

If only Chris was here. Trillory disliked chatting with strangers, but she could talk to her twin for hours. He had studied more about history and politics than she could ever learn, so he would know how to explain what was happening.

With a sigh, she wandered towards the balcony and looked out at the pouring rain. Chris was gone. There had been nothing she could do to save him.

She pushed through the doors and onto the balcony.

Lady Joline—the graceful socialite who tried to mentor Trill in courtly manners—was distracted with official business as ambassador from the Diamond Isles. She'd gotten a message from her government this morning and had locked herself in her room to write a response. She would be leaving soon to follow the duke to the capital.

For once Trillory had the afternoon to herself, and she planned to enjoy it.

Striding across the balcony, she leaned against the stone balustrade, inches from the rain. She would have preferred to be outside, exploring the grounds, but Joline had insisted on her staying out of the rain.

Of course she saw the wisdom in this. Even besides escaping the threat of a cold, none of the maids would have appreciated the puddle she would make coming in from this downpour.

The rain made it impossible to see anything more than a few yards away, much less the city of Charlon that rested below. But she still couldn't resist reaching out her hand to feel the cool spray of water on her fingers. She smiled. Quickly she glanced behind her and then pulled back her hand. Tilting it forward, she watched as the water on it collected into a large drop and rolled off, launching itself straight out and back into the rain.

She ran her now-dry hand through her hair, and turned to continue exploring. The manor was quite big, and Trill had barely seen half of it.

She wandered down one of the branching halls. The architecture of the duke's manor was marvelous—especially the north wing, which seemed to be the oldest part of the building. Trill wondered if even the king's palace could match it. Of course, there was a rumor that Charlon had once been the capital, so this would have belonged to the king.

Not that she minded the oversizing. It was nice to be alone. Even the servants weren't here today.

She pushed open the first door. The room only held one simple bed tucked in the corner, with a chest at its end, and a small table and seat by the window. A smaller door led to a closet. Had it not been raining, she would have opened the window and tried to get some air circulating. She had always disliked rooms—whether in use or not—without proper air flow.

But it was raining, and she left shortly. She found nothing in the next three rooms and was just opening a fifth door when someone spoke.

"They're all the same. And if there was anything special, I would know."

Trill spun to face the voice, and the door clacked loudly shut behind her. She found herself facing Eric, the duke's son.

She couldn't help blushing a bit, which was rare for her. How long had he been watching?

Though she had seen him several times in the weeks since she'd arrived, she had not actually talked to Eric. He must think she was daft. No normal person would be so absorbed with checking empty, stuffy rooms as not to notice someone walking up behind her.

She dropped a quick curtsy, and murmured under her breath, "Sir Eric."

He bowed slightly. "Lady Trillory. Tell me, how have you been enjoying your stay here?"

"Very well. I'm honored that your father welcomes me so warmly."

"He's always had a fondness for your family." He smiled down at her. "Would you like me to escort you anywhere?"

"It is not necessary."

"I insist. I would not leave you to wander alone on such a dreary day as this."

Eric extended his arm, practically sealing the deal with the motion.

Trill's shoulders slumped a bit. She would rather have kept exploring.

"Very well, then. I'd been planning to return to my quarters soon, anyway."

"Are you sure you wouldn't prefer the warmer atmosphere of the hall?" His eyebrows pulled into a puzzled frown, but his smile remained.

"I–I'm sure. I want to rest before tonight's party."

He nodded. "Of course."

She took his arm, and they started back to the main wing. They didn't talk much. She was relieved when the walk was over.

❧ 5 ❧

Terrin

Terrin sighted a squirrel. In one smooth movement she raised her bow, aimed, and fired. The squirrel, who had been busily snacking on a nut, came alert at the twang of her bow, but she had expected the reaction. A millisecond later, the arrow slammed into its left eye.

She started forward to collect her kill. She hadn't hunted since the previous fall, so she should have felt some sort of joy. But instead she could only chide herself for not shooting that well earlier. If she had been faster, if she had just taken down the wolf before it reached Arnold...

She removed the arrow, wiped it on the grass, and then started to clean the squirrel.

Behind her, she heard a twig snap. A twig more akin to a small branch, by the sound of it. Terrin froze, then slowly turned her head towards the sound. Seeing nothing through the underbrush, she stood, knife in hand.

There! She caught a glimpse of a face—an old woman with

angry eyes, dried mud on her face and in her hair. A swamp woman? But even as Terrin registered her appearance, the woman was gone.

Terrin took two steps forward and stared at the now-vacant space for several minutes. Her mind told her she must be crazy—they were in northwest Xell, and the swamp was far to the south. Her instinct told her to get away, head back to camp. And her curiosity bade her to investigate.

There was another snap, and she spun, looking for the woman. This time she saw a wraith slinking out from under a thicket. Its flat, disk-shaped head with its yellow-green eyes stared at her from barely a yard away, and its elbows jutting up above its body gave it an awkward look.

"Hello there," she said slowly, tightening her grip on the knife.

She'd been attacked by a wraith once, and though every schoolbook claimed they were peaceful creatures, she didn't trust them.

The wraith lunged forward. She moved into a fighting stance, but the wraith was already backing away. Its mouth seemed to be pulled back into a wide grin—and in its teeth was her freshly caught squirrel.

"Drop that!" Terrin said, stepping forward.

The wraith hissed as it straightened its legs. In a few seconds it went from being inches from the ground to being the size of a large pony. Terrin stared at the beast. She had never seen any animal do such a thing before, and she couldn't help taking a step back.

The wraith's grin seemed to grow even larger as it shrank back to its normal, flat position. It turned and scuttled away through the underbrush.

"Stinking thief," Terrin called after it, then sighed.

Glancing reluctantly back at where she had seen the woman disappear, she turned and headed away from both the wraith and the woman. She would have to settle her curiosity another day. She didn't want to go back to camp empty-handed, but any nearby prey would have been scared off by the noise.

She had been stalking quietly through the woods for only a few minutes when the smell of blood and rotting meat touched her nose. Dropping even lower into a crouch, she moved upwind towards the scent.

She didn't travel far before she found the scene of a battle. Six wolves lay around the trampled clearing, some torn almost beyond recognition. At first she thought two wolf packs had been fighting for territory. But she noticed a few unfamiliar tracks, too big for wolves or a wildcat, but not the right shape for a bear.

Then it struck her: the wraith.

With new interest, she stepped out of the shadows to examine the fight scene closer. There were more of the strange tracks. Two wraiths, at least, maybe more? She had never heard of wraiths traveling in a pack. The battle appeared to have been one-sided, since no wraiths had fallen. The tracks were so jumbled that it would take some time to work out exactly what had happened.

"The wraiths entered over here. They fought for a while, and then the last of the wolves fled."

Terrin spun to face the voice, sliding her knife free.

A forest woman was leaning against a tree, her arms crossed.

"The wraiths have grown more aggressive recently," she continued. "I can't pretend to understand their habits, but many of the territorial creatures are being driven away. Guess this wolf pack decided to fight."

A smile spread across Terrin's face, and she sheathed her knife as fast as she had drawn it. "Dyani!"

⁓ 6 ⁓

Brayden

Brayden jumped to his feet as the library door opened. With a flick of his wrist, he tossed the book on dragon myths he'd been reading to the table. The book flew, spinning once, and struck the stack of unread books, sending them to the floor. He glanced at the scattered books, then looked back up into the surprised, though quickly turning to frustrated, face of Mason. Mason was the king's chamberlain, Brayden's tutor in all but the art of war, and far too easily annoyed by the young prince's clumsiness.

Brayden dropped to his knees and started to pick up the books, keeping his head down to hide his strawberry cheeks.

Mason was a second cousin three times removed, or something of that sort. But he'd been selected for his post not for his blood, but for his authoritativeness and orderliness. His eclectic knowledge helped, too.

"My lord. Stand yourself up properly this moment. The servants can take care of that mess—bah, how you manage it, I do not know. Nearly a man grown, you should be dignified, self-confident, displaying poise suited to your position. Regardless, you are wanted in the council chamber this moment. I'll take care of this, you must hurry. Straighten your shirt before you go in. Pity you haven't time to change it."

Brayden stood and smoothed out his shirt. He bowed deeply, and Mason opened his mouth to start again, thought better of it, and merely said, "Go."

Brayden had avoided the council room since he was eight, when he had somehow—even he wasn't sure what he'd done—torn down one of the tapestries of King Miles, burying himself and several nobles in its heavy folds. Now he kept far away, except for special occasions.

He ran down the hall, managing to avoid any real mishaps, though he did nearly knock over a suit of armor rounding a corner in haste. Upon arriving at the door he straightened his shirt once more, brushed his moppy brown bangs out of his face, rubbed his hands together, and stepped into the room.

All of the major landholders were either there or had sent a representative. Currently they stood in small groups, talking quietly to one another. At the head of the room, his older brother Tyler stood on Father's right, tall and proud—the type of proud that demands respect, not the haughty kind—though a furious scowl covered his face. The queen sat in her smaller throne to the king's left, and her gaze latched onto Brayden as soon as he entered. A warm smile spread over her face.

Taking a deep breath, Brayden marched forward to the half-moon of clear space in front of his father, and bowed deeply. He raised his head just enough to see his father, but held the bow.

The king nodded.

"Come here, Brayden," he said, gesturing to his direct right.

Brayden frowned. It felt awkward to step between his father

and Tyler, but he obeyed.

"Brayden, tell me what you think of the incident with South Raec."

A hand seemed to tighten around Brayden's throat. He forced himself to breathe, running everything he knew of the incident over in his head, painfully aware that all attention had turned to him.

Why would his father ask a question like this, here?

"I think," he started slowly, but quickly sped up, "that though the evidence seems to show that it was an attack by South Raecans, we should not be too hasty to assume that the government of South Raec means to pick up hostilities."

One of the nobles started to protest, but Brayden ignored him and continued, his eyes squeezing shut against the watching faces.

"It would be best to send an envoy of peace to the king of South Raec, someone who would show your trust in his good nature. To ask what they know of the attack."

Brayden opened his eyes again and stared back into his father's stern eyes.

The king turned to look over the nobles.

Brayden followed his gaze. Duke Grith was the only noble who stood out—the only one ignoring the whispers that ran around the court. His face was smooth, expressionless, watching the king.

"And," the king continued, turning his gaze back to Brayden. "Who would you send on this important, but rather risky, mission?"

Brayden's head swung back to face his father quickly. Perhaps too quickly, as dizziness set in. *Please don't stutter.* He swallowed.

"My lord, I would send—"

Tyler's voice exploded from nowhere as he stepped forward to address the king. "Father, you— It's far too dangerous to send anyone of importance. A normal courier would be more than adequate. Let the current ambassador make inquiries. We dare not risk such a loss if anything should go awry!"

Brayden almost jumped at his brother's outburst, which set his skin to crawling. A sudden silence settled over the room, leaving Brayden feeling more claustrophobic than before, though he knew their eyes were no longer on him.

The king, however, seemed slightly amused. "And do you see no good in your brother's thoughts?"

"I see that any envoy important enough to show our trust would make a great hostage, should that trust be ill-founded. And South Raec's reaction might go the other way. They may take our action as a threat."

Brayden saw concern on his brother's face and realized that Tyler was pleading with their father.

The queen reached out and gripped her husband's arm.

The king nodded at her, then stood and needlessly raised his hand for the attention of the nobles.

"I thank you all for joining us today. I value all your opinions and advice," he started.

Only Brayden heard Tyler say one last pleading, "Father," under his breath.

"I have made my decision," the king continued, "and I trust that all of you will respect it."

Brayden scanned the nobles. Though they kept their faces straight, Brayden could sense anticipation. The duke smiled grimly.

"Prince Brayden shall be sent as emissary to South Raec, to assess the situation and to serve alongside Ambassador Gillian Fredrico in negotiating for peace."

Brayden almost fainted.

❧ 7 ❧

Nora

"Pleasure to meet you, Dyani of Xell," said Nora, studying the willowy woman before her.

"And you, Nora of Yorc." Dyani returned a quick appraisal, and then turned to Arnold, who was leaning back against a tree trunk. They exchanged greetings.

Then Dyani's eyes fell to his wrist, which was covered in blood-stained cloth. "We should take him to my village. Is it safe to move him?"

Nora nodded. "It sh—"

"It's not my legs that are hurt!" Arnold said, pushing himself to his feet with his good hand. He stood tall, broad-shouldered, with his eyes flashing a challenge.

Nora could tell exactly why he made such a good knight. She couldn't help smiling as she said, "As I was saying, it should be fine."

Dyani also seemed pleased—and amused—at his reaction.

"Good. I'll help pack up your camp."

෪

Arnold

As Nora and a forest man carefully cleaned the wound, applied a fine paste, and bandaged his wrist, Arnold couldn't help feeling like a child being fussed over by his mother for a skinned knee. Then the two healers made him drink a thick, bitter tea, admonished him to rest, and left him alone in the dim hut.

It was dry and comfortable, and a breeze moved in through the hanging cloth that sufficed for a door. The building was small and looked old, but as far as he could tell it was sturdy. The air smelled strongly of the herbs that lined the shelves.

He shifted slightly on the hanging cot, which bounced up and down, making him stiffen. He most definitely preferred sleeping on solid ground to this swaying monstrosity.

He considered slipping out of the hut to explore the village. But the town was small, and he had a feeling the sharp-faced healer would not approve. He turned his thoughts instead to Terrin.

Best he could tell, this was one of the nearest villages to Terrin's own, and Terrin had visited it often as a child. The woman, Dyani, appeared to be an old family friend. He smiled. Terrin must be happy to see familiar faces, he thought. She had been the least keen of them to travel with Chris. Arnold wondered vaguely where she was, as he shut his eyes. Probably catching up with her friends.

"I expected you to be pacing like a caged lion."

Arnold opened his eyes to see Terrin standing over him. He stared up at her for a moment.

Then he said, "Have you ever seen a caged lion?"

"Well, no."

"Then you can't know that it would pace."

"Maybe," she said dryly. "But the point is, I expected you to be pacing."

"And face the wrath of your healer friend? No thanks," he said with a small chuckle.

"I thought you were the one who was going to go off and face dragons without so much as a blink. This wound must be serious."

"Yes, well, dragons are mythical. You forest folk are just as fierce and quite real."

"Well, then, perhaps you had better obey orders and rest."

She pulled the room's only chair over next to the cot and settled herself in it.

"And of course, it falls to me to make sure you behave. You never can trust a caged lion."

❧ 8 ❧

Christopher

The Dark Forest loomed before them, the trees crowding close to each other, surrounded by deep shadows. Marc snorted as Chris urged him closer and pawed the ground when they stopped a few feet away.

Thomas gazed into the woods. Chris watched him out of the corner of his eye, wishing he could read the man's expression.

Finally Thomas spoke. "Certainly a cheery looking place. We aren't going through there, are we?"

Chris shook his head. "Of course not. We need to go farther south, to the boundary of Xell. We can cut east there."

Thomas half smiled. "Good. The stories are probably far-fetched, but who knows what's in there."

Chris shrugged. "I wouldn't be quick to dismiss the stories," he said. "The tales of King Miles are true. Why not these ones?"

"King Miles is a historical figure. Dark Forest stories are myths. Who ever heard of trees that can read minds or drive people insane?"

"Maybe. Who ever heard of riddles that can only be read by certain people, or dreams that offer guidance?"

"Actually, there are many versions of the King Miles story that say he was the only one who could read the riddles. Most dismiss this, since the idea of magic that can 'choose' people seems… unlikely. Also, since he supposedly traveled alone, how could he test it? But there are never any mentions of dreams." Thomas paused. "I suppose we know the truth now."

"Perhaps when this is over, you can go correct the stories," said Chris, turning Marc southward.

"I would like that," murmured Thomas.

Chris glanced over his shoulder, and saw Thomas smiling and absentmindedly rubbing his horse's neck.

"We should get going," Chris said, nudging Marc into a trot.

Chris had considered going through the Dark Forest, simply to avoid the risk of being seen. His month of grace was running out, probably already gone—he had lost track of days in the mountains. But no one would find him in there. After all, even the forest people refused to enter those woods.

The legends varied from telling to telling. Some said giant monsters roamed in the darkness, others warned of trees that came alive, and still others told of an aura that drove men crazy. What the tales did agree about was that people who entered that forest never came out again—except for the occasional "brave and pure knight."

Whatever was beyond the shadows, Chris didn't feel like testing those stories right now.

They rode in silence. As the ground rose, they slowed the horses to a walk. The trees sank below them. They found a narrow path headed east through the forest of Xell, following the edge of a cliff that towered over the Dark Forest.

When the path widened into a grassy clearing, Thomas nudged his horse forward to walk beside Marc.

"Did you know that King Miles didn't originally live in Coricstead? During the war, his parents died, and after the war his sister married someone from a small town—nobody even remembers what it was called. Since she was the only family he had left, he moved there with her. But then, because he was a hero and their new king, they changed the town's name, and it became the new capital."

"I didn't know Miles had a sister," said Chris.

"She never got involved in court life. It's quite possible, though, that there are still some of his sister's descendants living there."

For a few minutes, the air was quiet except for the thumping of the horse's hooves against the ground.

Finally Chris twisted to look at Thomas and said, "Why did you tell me that?"

"Well, if I was following Miles's footsteps, I'd like to know more about him. And I always thought that knowing he had a family he loved made him more human."

"Oh."

"Also, I admit I was trying to distract you, and perhaps coax you out of your shell. The only words you've said since we left my house are things like, 'We'll camp here,' and 'We'll go that way.' You have a lot on your mind. You just met me, and I doubt you want to share your problems with an old man, but mulling on your own thoughts for too long is never good. You should talk more, or at least listen."

Chris reined his horse to a stop.

Thomas did the same beside him and caught his gaze.

They stood there for a moment, then Chris's shoulders slumped, and he said, "It'll be dark soon. We can talk over supper."

A smile spread across Thomas's face. He said, "You know, being a healer isn't all herbs and physical sickness—that's just the easy part."

ᚨ 9 ᚨ

Trillory

Trill silently slipped out of the dining hall into the garden and away from the music of the party. She'd never been one for dancing, and this had become her usual retreat. She had thought the near-nightly socializing would end when the duke left last week, but Eric seemed determined to continue the tradition. Many of the remaining courtiers, including Joline, were to depart the next morning, for home or for the capital. But tonight they were all enjoying the party.

The last hints of sunset lingered over the town, evidence of the approaching summer. But the lamps in the garden were already lit, and some of the flames sparkled on the small pond. Trill had always enjoyed water, the smooth way it flowed, the crystal sounds, the way a rainstorm could change from calm to vicious and then fade away. Even the air seemed fresher around water.

Someone tapped her shoulder, and Trill spun to face the intruder. She was surprised to see Eric.

She dropped a curtsy.

He bowed his head. "Would you join me in the next dance?"

"Will it make you stop sneaking up on me?" She grinned.

Eric laughed. "Maybe you should pay more attention to your surroundings. But I suppose that I could make an extra effort."

He extended his arm, and she took it.

As they entered the room and waited for the music to start, she realized how short she was next to him. She was tall for a woman, matching Chris in height, but Eric was nearly a head taller.

"I feel like I know everyone here but you," he said. "We've talked, what, twice? The first day that you joined us, and then this afternoon."

"I suppose I'm used to the country life. There have been so many people to meet since I arrived, sometimes it seems over-whelming."

"It's hard to believe you didn't get through meeting everyone in the first week, with Joline as your guide. Though I do hear that you are a bit of a loner."

The music started, and she let him lead her into the dance. "I'm just not used to all the people and their gossiping. At my father's court, there was rarely anyone but family, servants, and a few soldiers."

"I hear your mother has been very ill."

Trill raised an eyebrow. "Surely Anthony has kept the duke informed of our mother's health."

"Sorry," he said.

Trill immediately regretted her tartness, and they danced in silence for several minutes.

She nibbled the edge of her lip, then spoke. "Mother has been ill for a while, now. We have one of the best healers constantly at her side, and Father hopes that one day she might recover. But she has little strength. I'm afraid I don't expect much change."

"And how did she react to the news of her youngest's actions?"

"We thought it best not to tell her." Trill tried to control the sudden chill in her voice and hoped he would not pursue the subject of Chris.

"Surely she'll notice his absence?"

Of course not, she thought sadly. "She sometimes goes for several weeks without seeing us, even if we visit daily."

"I see. I'm sorry."

Trill took the short pause to change the subject. "Do you remember your mother?"

"No. Though my father often tells me that I take after her."

"In looks or in personality?"

"I'm not sure. I do have her eyes, but beyond that it is hard to tell."

Trill glanced up into his hazel eyes. She didn't know what his mother's eyes were like, but Eric's were most certainly not like his father's dark ones.

"And as to her personality," he continued, "I've been told very little. You have seen the picture of her?"

"I'm not sure. I haven't had much chance to look at the artwork, though what I have seen has been very well done, like the rest of the manor."

He chuckled. "With Joline as a guide, I'm not surprised. She does her job well and knows everyone, but she never has time for art. But that's beside the point: the best portrait of my mother is in the private section of the west wing, in the middle of the gallery between my father's chamber and mine. But there is also a very good tapestry to the immediate right of the grand entrance."

"Then your mother was indeed very beautiful."

"Hmm. Do you weave tapestries?"

"I must admit I never took much to needlework of any sort. I'm more of a gardener."

He nodded. "Of course, I cannot say I would enjoy needlework. But I have always found the use of colors interesting in all kinds of art. The way minute changes in the shading can make a scene look so realistic. Unfortunately, I have little talent with a brush."

"Yes, art can be fascinating to study. But I suppose I have always preferred natural things."

"Well, I hope you have enjoyed our gardens."

"Your fountain is very nice, and the arrangements are fine enough. Your men have certainly put a lot of work into the topiaries."

Eric narrowed his eyes at her. "You sound like you have seen better."

Trill blushed. "Well, I am probably biased, but I can't help but compare them to the gardens back home."

"Well then, hopefully one day I will see them and decide for myself."

He spoke the last part in a rush as the music ended and he guided her to the edge of the room.

"We should talk again soon, Lady Trillory."

"Please, call me Trill," she said impulsively.

They exchanged a bow and curtsy, and she watched as he walked away. She found herself pleasantly surprised. She had expected Eric to be haughty, like her brother Anthony, but now she wished she'd befriended him sooner.

$\backsim$ 10 $\backsim$

Brayden

"This is the chance to prove you are not a total klutz. Don't waste it." The words of his tutor rang through Brayden's head.

He had realized about four years ago that Mason really did want the best for him, but sometimes that fact was hard to remember. And, of course, what Mason thought was best, and what Brayden thought was best, were often two very different things. Now, though, they were agreed. Brayden had a chance not only to prove himself, but also to prevent a war. This trip could save lives and keep the peace his father and grandfather had worked so hard for.

When the king had announced that he would not be sending his eldest, but instead his youngest, to speak with the South Raecan king, Brayden had been ecstatic. He wasn't sure what had led his father to that decision, though Duke Grith had been the only noble who'd seemed at all pleased by the situation.

Outside a carriage awaited to carry him to the river where a ship would take him post-haste to South Raec.

Where the ambassador would no doubt order—unofficially, of course—that Brayden remain unobtrusive for the entirety of his stay.

Not that I care, Brayden told himself, tossing a simple white shirt into his bag.

He grinned. Had Mason been present he'd have scolded Brayden for not calling a servant to do 'such a menial task.' That was definitely a place where they disagreed—how much he should do for himself, and how much he should have servants do.

He quickly scanned his room for anything else he might need. Then he hoisted the bag onto his shoulders and walked out into the hall.

Where he nearly collided with Tyler.

Both the princes quickly moved back—Tyler with a single long step, whereas Brayden hopped back quickly, banging his elbow against the door frame. He gripped his elbow, grinding his teeth.

Tyler took a short breath and started talking as if nothing had happened. "Are you sure this is wise? If the South Raecans are planning to attack us—"

"Then they will not want to be rushed into it by killing me or the ambassador. It would be nigh impossible to keep news of that sort from getting back here."

"But they will want to be pushed into a treaty even less. If they were to break a newly-signed treaty, then even their closest allies would be reluctant to offer friendship."

"Neither will they dare to kill me in cold blood. If they are trying to start a war, they will either declare it openly or send me back without agreeing to anything."

"Brayden—"

"Tyler, please. I want to do this. It's what is best."

"It's what you think is best, but if you die..."

"Which I won't. Unless, of course, I catch some sort of exotic disease." Brayden tilted his head, letting his eyes glaze over, and considered this for a moment before continuing. "I suppose that is possible, since Colyth does quite a bit of trading. Do you think I'll have much time to—"

"It's not funny." Tyler's brow creased, and his hands gripped the edge of his shirt, rumpling the cloth.

"Tyler, please. If war breaks out, many will die. At most, I'm risking my freedom. And if I have a chance to stop a war, I don't mind risking that. If my trip turns out for naught, if the Raecs fight anyway, and... and Father dies—"

Brayden swallowed and started down the hall.

"I'm done arguing," he said. "Everyone is probably thinking I've fallen down the stairs and am out cold. I know you care, but this is good for me."

Tyler shook his head and followed.

"I want peace as much as you," Tyler said, "but this isn't the only way. Probably not even the best way— You're only sixteen, Brayden. Don't act like you know what's best." His voice was rising.

Brayden ignored him.

Tyler followed behind, but before he could come up with another argument, they were interrupted. Earl Diard Fredrico rose from one of the small benches placed sporadically around the castle. As soon as he was up, he bowed deeply, and Brayden nearly missed seeing the paper he held.

The two princes bowed their heads in return. Then Tyler spoke. "Earl Fredrico, how nice to see you."

Brayden repeated a similar greeting.

"I had not expected the honor of meeting both of you, my lords," said Diard. "I, uh..." He glanced at the elder prince, then carried on. "I merely wished to wish you good luck on your journey, Prince Brayden."

"Thank you," Brayden said, smiling at the Earl.

"I know I shouldn't ask, but the current ambassador is one of my sons. And I was wondering if you could pass along my greetings?"

Brayden realized the Earl had intended to ask this favor privately, not in front of the crown prince.

And the boy couldn't help but notice him fidget with the paper.

"Of course. I'd be glad to deliver that and any other message you might have for him."

"I do happen to have a letter. I had meant to send it on the next mail carrier, but if you'd be willing… I happen to have it right here."

Beside Brayden, Tyler gave a slight twitch. Brayden sent a quick glance at his older brother out of the corner of his eye, and was not surprised to find him smiling.

"Of course, Earl Diard," Brayden said. He accepted the letter with a formal nod. "Would you honor us with your company down to the courtyard?"

Of course the Earl could not refuse, and the three set off again. Now there was silence except for the tap, tap of Brayden's boots against the stone floor. The others wore soft leather shoes that made barely any noise.

❧ 11 ❧

Trillory

The chorus of farewells filled the air, and the carriages started pulling away. Trill wished she was in one of them. She'd sent a letter to Father asking that she might go home, as many of the nobles were doing. Her father had refused. Of course, he was trying to do what was best for her. The duke's manor had once been a castle, and it could still be defended if the war came to them. And her older brother Anthony, as one of Duke Grith's knights, was staying here in Charlon, though the duke himself was still with the king.

Trillory frowned. Anthony was Father's favorite, but he had a cruel streak, and she always did her best to avoid him. That would be harder than ever, now.

Lady Joline waved from the carriage window, finally on her way to join the duke in Coricstead. She had complained about having to wait for instructions from the Isles. As an ambassador, it was her job to be in the middle of things, and she worried that by the time she reached the capital, all the interesting stuff would be done and over with.

Joline was sure that if the Diamond Isles took sides in the coming war, it would join with North Raec, but Trill thought they would keep themselves out of the fray.

If there was a fray to join.

Which Trill hoped there wasn't.

The last carriage went through the gate and disappeared into the streets. Now the castle really did seem empty. Only the duke's knights remained, and a few of the ladies like Trill.

Perhaps finally there won't be a ball, thought Trill wryly, as she walked away from the courtyard.

She entered the garden. She'd rather be there than in the stuffy castle, quiet as it would finally be. She wished she had some clippers so that she could trim the small hedge maze. It would be nice to do some work she could really appreciate.

There was a cough from behind her, and she turned around to face Eric.

"Sir Eric!" she said, dropping a quick curtsy.

"Honestly," he said, "if I am to call you Trill, then you should drop the sir."

She smiled. "Just Eric then."

"No, Eric. No 'Just' about it."

Trill was confused. Had it been Arnold, she would have known it was a joke, but it was hard to tell with Eric.

Eric waited for a second, then sighed.

"Never mind. Shall we walk?" He gestured broadly to the whole garden. "I find if one stares at a single patch of flowers too long, one begins to see every little flaw. And I would hate for you to see all the flaws of our garden. Especially when you already think less of it than your own."

Trill resisted shrugging. She was sure Eric was trying to put a lighter mood on things, but she couldn't decide how best to respond.

"I suppose you're too late for that," she said. "I was already thinking of trimming your hedges. But we can walk."

He grinned. "Then I had best distract you. Our gardener takes a lot of pride in his hedges."

He offered his arm. She accepted it, allowing him to lead her away from the maze. She watched his face out of the corner of her eye. She couldn't help wondering why he kept going out of his way to talk to her. Perhaps he was just trying to be friendly. After all, when he was duke, he would want good relations with the other noble families.

They walked in silence for a minute.

Then he spoke again. "I should apologize."

"Whatever for?"

Trill stared at him, struggling to keep her mouth from falling open. She tried to think of something he should apologize for.

"For being so forceful about you leaving the north wing. I had my reasons, but they weren't enough to excuse my rudeness."

Trill considered this for a second. She agreed that he had seemed rather insistent. But she hadn't really thought of it as needing an apology. But he had offered one, so she nodded.

"Apology accepted."

Again there was a minute of silence.

Then he continued. "I'm also sorry I didn't seek you out earlier. I knew that I'd have to befriend you at some point, but I waited. And I'm sorry I did. I mean, what kind of duke am I to be, if I won't save a damsel from torture."

Trill arched an eyebrow. "You consider it torture to go without having met you?"

"No, I consider it torture to be Lady Joline's constant companion."

"You almost sound like you speak from experience."

"I do." He winced.

Trill couldn't help laughing a bit at his expression. He laughed, too, and something about him looked relieved.

"Well," Trill continued, "she is gone now. Though I feel sorry for the queen and her ladies."

He nodded.

Trill had not realized how long it took to walk around the entire garden, though she had seen all but the maze from a bird's-eye view. But she was beginning to see that Eric was a bit like Chris or Arnold, a potential friend. She had expected him to be more serious, bordering on angry, like Anthony.

Now that the laugh had put her at ease, she needed to clear the air.

"But we shouldn't make fun of Joline, you know. She can be a prattle, but she has good intentions."

Though as she said this, she couldn't help remembering that momentary gleam in Joline's eyes the day the king's messenger arrived. The woman had almost looked excited—but no, that was just her overactive imagination.

Eric nodded solemnly.

They walked for a while in silence, coming back around to the start of the path.

"Perhaps we should go in," she said. She was beginning to feel tense again.

"As you please," he answered. "By the way, I was thinking of organizing a small hunt. Nothing big, mostly a reason to ride around the countryside."

"I should like that, if you have a horse you can lend me. I'm afraid I left mine at home."

"I'm sure we can find one to suit you. Would you like to look at the options?"

Trillory's stomach twinged, and she glanced up at the sun, surprised at how much time had passed. "Perhaps after lunch."

Eric glanced up as well, and then nodded.

"Yes, after lunch would be good." He smiled. "Well then, I look forward to it, Trill."

❧ 12 ❧

Terrin

Standing at the edge of a cliff, Terrin stared down on green trees that faded into the distance, so thick that you could hardly tell they were leaves and not grass. From up here, it didn't look too spooky, but she knew this was the very edge of the Dark Forest.

To her right, a river rushed over the cliff and crashed down into a small clearing, but the sound seemed dull, muffled by a steady, buzzing hum. Below, a stream from the waterfall's base flowed away into the trees.

Beside it lay a black body, cruelly twisted.

She was locked to the spot not by fascination with the body, but by the strange prickling sensation along her back. She had felt that cold tingle before.

Magic.

Four spirits moved out from the trees, pale figures gliding towards the carcass. They formed a half circle around it. Then they looked up at her.

Even from this distance, she could tell they were smiling.

Terrin put her arm out, trying to reach something to steady herself against, but found nothing.

She couldn't tear her eyes away, and though there were no words in the strange humming, she knew they were calling to her. They were pulling her forward, closer to the edge.

She felt her body sway forward.

Her mind screamed.

❧

"Terrin. Terrin?"

An insistent voice pulled her away from the cliffs and out of the dream. She woke to a headache and sore neck.

"It's morning," said Nora. She moved past Terrin, set a shallow wooden bowl on the small table, and then turned to Arnold's side. Slowly she started to pull back the bandages, her every move filled with intent. "Good to see you both got some sleep."

Terrin blinked, pushing away the dream—ineffectively—and rubbing at her temples.

"Not sure that was really sleep."

Using her hands she popped her neck, and then moved to rolling her shoulders. The dream was still vivid behind her eyelids, but the movement seemed to help.

Nora pulled the last of the bandages away, dropped them across Arnold, and turned to the bowl. Terrin watched with minor interest as Nora pulled a half-submerged cloth from the thick liquid.

Sighing, Terrin stood and walked across the room, swinging her arm up as high as she could into the air. She paused in front of the door and concentrated on stretching. As she finished getting out her kinks, she turned back towards Nora.

The Yorc girl was holding Arnold's arm in one hand, and the

washcloth in another, but she stood stiffly, her eyes locked on the wound.

"Nora?" Terrin asked, quickly stepping back to Nora's side. "What's wrong?"

Nora shook her head with quick short jerks, then turned her head to look at Terrin.

"I think it's infected."

Terrin arched her neck to see the wound clearly over Nora's shoulder, and immediately wished she hadn't. Though the light was dim, she could see the heavy bruising around torn skin that opened to red, live flesh. Bile rose in her throat.

The cloth at the door rustled as Healer Koresh stepped into the medicine hut. Terrin backed away from the hammock to give him room. She felt the wall behind her and leaned against it, glad for the support.

Arnold flinched as the healer took his hand and ran a finger over the skin. Koresh lifted Arnold's other hand off the bed and held it next to the wounded one, turning them to examine all sides.

Nora put a hand on Arnold's forehead. "You have a bit of fever," she said. "Your body is trying to fight the infection."

"There is definite swelling here," Koresh said. "We are fortunate, however, in that the redness has not spread far above the wrist."

He bent over, holding Arnold's hand near his nose.

Nora watched him, frowning.

He straightened up, met her gaze, and nodded.

"We have two options," he said. "We could remove his hand now, and lose the minimal amount."

Terrin squeezed her eyes shut.

"Or we could try to clean out the infection," Koresh continued, "but risk losing more of the arm. In my own opin—"

"Do it now," said Arnold, and even without seeing him, Terrin could tell there was fire in his eyes.

She turned and stumbled outside, but she couldn't bear to go far. Clutching the doorway with one hand, she pressed her head against the wall of the medicine hut. The rough wood scraped her cheek.

"As I was saying," continued the healer, obviously annoyed, "it is my opinion that, since our medicines have failed to stop the infection from setting in, we can hardly expect them to remove it. I understand that this might be hard to acce—"

This time, Nora interrupted him. "Okay, let's get it over with. I'll tie off his arm. Where is your bone saw?"

Terrin almost smiled as she imagined the healer's frozen face. After all, it was one thing for an eighteen-year-old girl to have healing knowledge, quite another for her to be willing without hesitation to cut off her friend's hand.

Then her stomach flipped.

What would happen now?

What if the operation went badly?

Or—

No, she thought. *Just assume it will go well, and concentrate on the practicalities.*

But those thoughts were no more encouraging: Once Arnold lost his hand, who knew when he'd be able to travel? How much could he do without a left hand? He was trained as a warrior, but how would he hold a shield?

Dyani came around the hut and took in the situation at a glance. She took Terrin's arm and pulled her away.

"Come on, you should eat breakfast," she said softly. "They will be busy, and you would be in their way."

Terrin walked in a daze to Dyani's cottage. She stared out the window while the forest woman fixed her a plate of steaming eggs and sliced venison and poured them both a cup of cool water. Her thoughts kept turning to what was happening to Arnold. Every time, her imagination pictured something worse.

"Arnold is obviously important to you," Dyani said.

"He was my first friend among the plainsmen."

"I see."

Terrin met Dyani's eyes and saw her concern.

The older woman reached across to pat Terrin's hand. "Koresh knows his craft. He will take care of the boy."

They sat in silence. Dyani sipped her drink while Terrin picked at the food.

"Koresh's sleeping draught is strong," Dyani said. "Arnold will sleep for several hours after they are done. You need to distract yourself. Maybe you should hunt, or—"

Terrin's dream popped to mind, and she straightened up.

"I'm going to the cliff—the one by the Dark Forest."

Dyani cocked her head. "I thought you hated it up there?"

"I've been having dreams about it, that's all. I just… I have to go see. And it's not like I'm needed here."

"I was thinking more along the lines of visiting your parents. But if you feel this is important—"

"Will you tell the others where I've gone?" Terrin asked.

Dyani's eyebrows rose, but she gave a slow nod. "Very well."

Terrin shoveled the last bite of eggs down her throat and took a long drink of water. The thought of going near the Dark Forest, and the spirits who lived within, sent shivers down her spine. But the idea of investigating her dream gave her a sense of purpose, and she clung to that.

As she reached the door, she paused and turned to look back

at Dyani. "Don't mention the part about the dreams. Please."

"Worried that they'll think you're insane?" Dyani smiled. "I will merely say that you felt inclined."

Terrin returned the smile, but didn't voice the thought that immediately crossed her mind: *No, I'm not worried about what they will think. I'm worried because I think I'm insane.*

ӧ 13 ӧ

Christopher

Great. How had he forgotten that there was a waterfall here? Was there even supposed to be a waterfall here? Chris shut his eyes trying to remember back to geography lessons. But all he could see, or rather hear, was a little voice saying, *Terrin would know.*

He glared inwardly at himself. Terrin was exactly where she should be—on her way home, away from danger.

Besides, of course the waterfall was supposed to be here. It wasn't like someone could magically move a river this big, just to block his way. Still, he was beginning to wonder if Nora had been right when she said all four of them would be needed for this quest. He had not had another dream since just after finding the second riddle, and the riddle itself made no sense to either him or Thomas.

It's too late now, he thought. *I'll just make the best of it.*

"We'll rest here for a while," he said. "Then we can head upstream to find a ford."

"Very well," Thomas said, and they both dismounted. "I'd say it's about lunch time, wouldn't you?" he added as he bent to hobble his horse.

Chris glanced at the sun. "A bit past, by the time it's prepared. And this is as good a place to stop as any."

"Best we hurry then. I'll fetch the firewood."

Chris stared across the river. The water shone as it rushed along towards the drop, and he imagined the fall must look beautiful from down below. Fetching their water skins, he knelt to fill them while Thomas gathered wood for a fire.

"I'll make a stew," Chris called over his shoulder.

Cooking wasn't a talent of his, but the old man had decided he should learn. He cleared a spot for the fire and set up the pot holder Thomas had brought with him. He pulled some jerky from his saddlebag and began to cut it into bite-size chunks.

Thomas dropped an armful of wood and came to look over his shoulder.

"Looks tasty," Thomas said. "I saw a bit of a pool upstream. Should be able to get some cattail roots. Not quite potatoes, but they'll do."

Chris nodded without looking up.

Ha, he thought. Here he was: banished, traveling off-road, avoiding towns, knowing that anyone he met could hand him over to be locked away or worse. Yet he had time to be schooled in the ways of cooking. That would have made Arnold laugh.

He turned his attention to starting the fire.

The stew had just started to simmer when he heard a low growl and looked around. Thomas stood at the edge of the clearing, his feet covered in mud and his arms filled with roots. He was staring west, the way they'd come, where something moved in the undergrowth just inside the forest.

Three somethings.

Chris gasped as the beasts crept into the light, crouching low in the long grass, the tips of their thick tails twitching back and forth. Yellow, cat-like eyes caught the light, almost glowing against the black skin.

"Wraiths," he said, remembering the name from his time at school.

The middle one paused, drawing in a long breath. Then it let out a growl.

Slowly reaching down to grab the sword at his waist, Chris stared back at the creatures and swallowed. He wasn't thrilled at the prospect of stabbing through those scales.

The middle wraith seemed to be the leader. It glanced at Thomas for a moment, and then turned back to Chris, once again pulling in a long breath.

Then it leaped.

As the beast sailed through the air, front legs stretched out to show long, curving claws, Chris dived away from the fire. The wraith landed where he had been. It snarled and turned towards him, showing its sharp white teeth.

Chris's sword had landed beneath him when he fell. Before he could free it, the wraith lunged at him, claws lashing towards his face.

Thomas charged into the wraith with his shoulder, knocking it off balance, buying Chris enough time to get to his feet. But little more, for a second wraith was racing towards them.

Chris tugged his sword from where it had stuck in the ground and spun to face this new attack. The creature was almost on him, and as he turned, his sword hit it across the nose. It barely made a scratch, but the wraith pulled up short, shaking its head.

He struck again, this time aiming for the eye, but the beast ducked surprisingly flat to the ground and then lunged forward. Chris dodged left and swung his sword at its neck. The sword bounced off the hard scales, and in return the beast's tail whipped around and struck him in the side, knocking him back to the ground.

His side throbbed as he scrambled to a crouch, turning towards the wraith. The wraith was standing over him, its paw posed to strike. The claws were clearly visible, as was a thin webbing between the toes. Chris struck quickly, cutting at the webbing.

The wraith pulled back and hissed, and Chris rose to his feet, striking again across the nose with all the force he could muster. It backed away, stumbling and shaking its head, spraying drops of blood.

Scanning the clearing quickly, Chris spotted Thomas in battle with both of the other wraiths, showing amazing nimbleness. But he was being pushed back toward the river, and Chris could see a bad scratch on his cheek.

Then one of the wraiths stumbled into the fire, and as it flailed in pain, its tail struck the stew pot, sending it flying towards Chris.

He dodged away from the scalding liquid and found himself once again face to face with the wounded wraith. It snapped at him, and he stepped backward. It swung its claws and again he moved back. When the beast lunged again, he jumped to the right, but he had forgotten the flailing tail, which caught his legs and knocked him sprawling to the ground.

Momentarily stunned, he lay gasping on the ground, unable to lift his head more than a few inches. A clawed paw pressed against his right shoulder, pinning him down. Pain shot through his arm, and he was sure his old cut had reopened. He could feel the wraith's breath as it sniffed at his left ear. He jerked his left arm back and felt his elbow connect with the beast's great head. The weight of the wraith's paw lightened just enough for Chris to drag himself free.

As he slid, he twisted back and struck his fist against the beast's jaw. It reared its head, hissing. Chris scrabbled backward. The beast shook its head, but the dazed look passed quickly. Its muscles tensed to lunge again.

And then an arrow struck the soft, loose skin that Chris supposed was part of its ear.

The wraith made a loud sound, something between a hiss and a howl. Its head whipped around to face the new attacker, and Chris couldn't help following its gaze.

And choked.

❧ 14 ❧

Nora

"How are you feeling today?" Nora asked as she entered the healer's hut.

Arnold had shifted himself to be sitting up in the hammock, leaning into the wall. His left forearm lay across his lap, the stump wrapped in white linen.

"Fine," he said. "Am I allowed to get up yet?"

"Patience, sir knight! Let's take a look."

She set down her bowl of water and reached for his arm. Gently she unwrapped the outer cloth and pulled at the dressing, sponging it with water where it stuck. Arnold watched her, clearly trying to look nonchalant. He had slept through the last time she checked his wound, so this would be the first time he saw his stump.

"We need to soften the dressing, so it won't pull at your skin," she explained.

The more he knows, she thought, *the less helpless he will feel.*

"You might as well pay attention, so you can tend to this yourself. I don't plan on being your servant."

Arnold gave a short laugh, but his jaw clenched.

Nora tugged again at the dressing, and this time it came off cleanly. The skin looked bruised but not inflamed. Good. She picked up a new cloth and dipped it in the water.

"Don't scrub hard when you wash. Rub gently, to clean and stimulate the skin. And check for drainage, redness, or new swelling."

She put a clean dressing on and wrapped the outer cloth around, pulling it snug to reduce swelling.

"You need to tuck in the ends to hold it in place, like so." She pulled the cloth back off and held it out. "Would you like to try?"

He reached over and fumbled with the cloth, then dropped his hand in frustration.

"My fingers are too thick for such work."

"No, but it does take practice." She fastened the wrap again. "You'll learn. How is the pain?"

"I can handle it."

She smelled the sticky-sweet tang of a healing brew. Koresh came into the room, tea mug in hand.

"Of course you can handle it," he said. "But do not be stupid. Untreated pain will only lengthen the healing process. Here, drink."

Arnold scowled at the cup.

"Will it make me sleep? I'd rather have the pain."

"He wants to walk around," Nora explained.

The healer nodded.

"Surgery strains the entire body system," he said. "But no one ever listens until they feel it for themselves. One-half hour only, and stay with him."

He handed her the tea and left.

Nora turned back to Arnold and placed her free hand on her

hip. "So," she said, "if I let you get up, do you promise not to run off and search for Terrin?"

The day before, when he had woken up after the operation and heard that Terrin was gone, Arnold had been worried she was pulling a Chris and abandoning them.

He snorted. "As if I would even know how. I never had to take tracking classes. Besides, Terrin can take care of herself."

"Then, sure. Drink this first, and you can walk. Just don't put any pressure on your wound."

"Finally!" he said, swinging his legs to the side of the hammock. He stumbled a bit, but Nora grabbed his right arm and helped him get his balance.

"That hanging cot will be the death of me," he said, "with all its bouncing about. Do you know how hard it was just to sit up in it?"

He reached for the cup and drained it, grimacing at the taste.

Nora pulled back the doorway to let him escape into the sunshine.

Terrin

The wraith turned away from Chris, and Terrin pulled back another arrow. Even as the beast charged, she forced herself to take a second to breathe. Focus. Release. The arrow struck just above the wraith's right eye.

The creature pulled up short, throwing its head back. Rising on its hind legs, it howled.

Terrin quickly nocked another arrow. This time, she struck just where the beast's leg met its body.

The wraith quickly flattened itself, then hissed as the movement drove the arrow in deeper. She heard the shaft snap and began to nock a fourth arrow. Yellow eyes glared at her for a moment, then the beast turned and ran, staggering each time it landed on the wounded leg.

Smiling, Terrin turned her bow to where two more wraiths were circling an older man.

"Hey!" she shouted.

Both wraiths spun toward the sound, and she released her

arrow. The point only nipped her target's ear, but the beast stepped away from the man, hissing.

And bounded towards Terrin, stretching up to full height as it did so.

❧

Christopher

Chris watched as Terrin released another arrow, which struck the hard scales and deflected. Then he heard Thomas give a small cry. He turned and saw the older man still in battle with one of the monsters. Bright red scratches streaked his arm.

Chris jumped up and ran towards him, looping out of reach of the beast's tail. He came in from the side and struck its flank. The blow was too weak to break the armored skin, but the wraith turned to face this new attacker.

Thomas darted forward, slashing at the side of its head. The creature pulled back, hissing, tilting its head from one man to the other. Then, as Chris stepped forward to strike again, it turned and fled.

Chris couldn't help giving a long sigh of relief.

What about Terrin? He turned, raising his sword for one more fight.

She had circled around the third wraith and crouched only a couple feet from the cliff's edge. She slipped her bow around her quiver without looking away from the charging beast.

Chris froze. He would never get there in time.

Then Terrin moved. Just as the wraith took its final leap, she dove sideways, rolling smoothly and bouncing back to her feet. The wraith landed and slid, scrambling for purchase. Then it went over the edge. Its scream fell away into silence. Terrin stood and stepped back to the cliff, looking down after it.

Chris let out another sigh, and moistened his lips. Then he knelt to clean his sword before sheathing it.

When he stood, he saw Terrin still standing at the cliff's edge. She was swaying slightly, as if in a trance. She shivered, and then she put out one arm as if to catch something.

"Uhm," said Thomas softly from behind him. "That doesn't look like a good idea."

"Terrin?" Chris called.

As soon as he spoke, it was as if something snapped. She spun around to face him, all traces of the trance gone.

සා

Terrin

Chris was staring at her, and Terrin couldn't help glaring back. She hated the tingly chill of magic, and she was slightly in shock—not from the fight, but that she'd just reenacted her dream. She could still feel prickles from the four spirits below.

She glanced around the clearing. The old man was also staring at her. A dented pot lay several yards from the dying fire.

"Where's the other wraith?" she asked, throwing off the last effects of the spirits' magic.

"Gone." Chris waved his hand vaguely toward the forest. "Are you okay? Why are you here?"

Terrin's lips quirked into an almost-smile.

"Apparently I'm here to save your life. But don't suppose I expect any thanks."

"Er, thank you, Miss, uh, Terrin?" said the older man, glancing between Terrin and Chris.

Terrin almost laughed at his confusion.

Almost.

"But why were you here in the first place?" Chris said, frowning. "You're not supposed to be here."

"You are so…" Terrin pulled in a deep breath.

Then she crossed the clearing in a few long steps. As she took the final step she pivoted on the ball of her left foot, tightened her right hand into a fist, and struck Chris hard across the jaw.

He stumbled back automatically, raising his hand to rub the spot, and winced.

Terrin stood there breathing heavily for a second, until Chris met her gaze.

Then she finished her sentence.

"… frustrating! Entirely and completely frustrating. And irrational, and stupid and—"

He dropped his gaze.

"—bratty and childish and, and, and—"

"I'm sorry, Terrin," he said.

Terrin glared at him for a moment longer, but her mind had suddenly gone blank on insults. So instead, she hugged him as tightly as she could.

PART TWO

❧ 16 ❧

Terrin, 5 years earlier

"That's enough for now," Terrin murmured, pulling the shallow bowl of milk away, careful not to spill. The fox kit pressed its cold nose against Terrin's other hand. She smiled and ran her fingers along its soft fur, stopping short of the blanket that covered its lower body.

"Well, with an appetite like that, you must be feeling just fine," she said.

She had found the fox nearly starved to death, the rest of its litter already dead, a bit over a week ago. Either from luck or sheer stubbornness, it had recovered.

There was a slight rustle of cloth as someone entered. She could half guess who it was by the shadow he cast and the feeling of his presence.

"Can I pet it?" he said.

Sure enough, she recognized the warm voice. She glanced back and smiled, resisting the urge to jump up and hug the swamp man behind her.

"Zuen!" she said softly. This was the first time he'd stopped at her village since she'd returned from school.

The merchant knelt beside her and held out his hand towards the fox. Like all swamp-people, his skin had a gray complexion, but his hair was thicker than most. Laugh lines creased his face.

"I hear your brother has been helping you with this?"

"I've been doing most of the work, though." Terrin raised her chin and grinned. "And she likes me best."

"I'm sure," said Zuen, laughing softly. "So, what have you learned since I last saw you?" He asked.

"Mostly math, and history." Terrin wrinkled her nose.

"I thought you liked history."

"Not the way *they* tell it," she said. "It's so dry. And we don't get to languages till high school."

She caught her hair and pulled it back from her face.

"I wish you taught there, Zuen. You would like Arnold and Chris."

"I'm afraid that I would not fit in very well, though. And swamp tongue isn't the most popular of languages. You're rather unique in wanting to learn that."

"I still wish you were there." As far as she was concerned, he was a beehive of interesting knowledge.

She ran her hand along the fox's fur.

Then she stood. "Can you teach me more words before you leave? Or tell me some stories?"

"Of course." Zuen stood after her. "In fact, I was thinking I might even start you on some of the ancient dialect."

"Really?"

In her excitement, she neglected to keep her voice low. The fox yipped, darting under its blankets. She quickly dropped back to her knees.

"I'm sorry, baby." She reached a single finger gently under the covers. "I forgot myself. It's okay."

The fox's nose peaked out, sniffing the air. Terrin slid her eyes shut and started singing softly. There were no real words to her song, just soft cooing sounds. She half-sensed, half-heard Zuen slip out of the room. She continued to sing, softly, focusing out all other sounds. The nonsense syllables came to her mind instinctively, forming a rhythm that reminded her of something, but she didn't know what. Time ceased to exist as she shifted to that almost-unconscious state where one feels detached from the world.

Then something soft and wet bumped against her hands.

Her eyes slid open, and a smile spread over her face. The fox was pressed low, and its ears swiveled this way and that, but it was creeping into her lap. Slowly, she brushed her hand against its head. She continued to sing until it straightened its legs and bumped its head against her chest.

She laughed quietly, scratching the fox behind its ears.

"It's your naptime," she said after a minute. She reached to move the fox to its bed, but it turned and went on its own, tunneling under the blanket till just its nose peaked out.

As she stood, a tingle of pleasure ran up her spine.

Or was it pleasure?

Terrin's head snapped up, but the tingling sensation was gone. She stood there for a moment, trying to remember exactly what she had felt.

Then she whispered to the fox, "I probably imagined that."

Everything remained quiet in the dark house. She shrugged and turned to slip out the door. Zuen was waiting for her outside.

"You know," he said, "if you were half as gentle with people as you are with that fox, you'd have a lot more friends."

"Hmmph." Terrin tossed her head. "And what would be the fun of that?"

❧ 17 ❧

Trillory

"I suppose we should be heading back," said Magnolia, peering through the trees. "Pity. I had so hoped for some berries."

Trill gave a half-shrug in answer, but kept her gaze to the south. Absentmindedly she smoothed her divided skirt over her leggings.

"Wait! I think I see something," cried Magnolia.

This time Trill turned to look where the other lady was scrambling through the brush. Sighing, she followed. But still she felt that slight tingling sensation that had pulled her attention south.

The only thing she could describe it as, was magic.

Trill made herself ignore the feeling and attend to Magnolia's discovery.

"Ooh, the others will like these," Trill said.

She unslung a bag from her shoulder and started to open it, but stopped as she heard something snort. Magnolia opened her mouth, but Trill held up a hand to silence her.

A few seconds later, they saw a great, shaggy head break through the bushes.

A bear's head.

Then the rest of the bear, as it rose and sniffed at the air. Its head tilted sideways, and it stared down at them.

Trill glanced at Magnolia, who was shaking like a leaf.

"Run," Trill said.

Magnolia sprinted off into the woods, her split skirt twisting around her legs, snagging at the branches but being torn free quickly. Trill ran close behind her, glad they were in riding habits and not the long, courtly skirts.

The bear gave a roar, and soon the thumping of its great paws was nearly as loud as the sound of twigs snapping beneath her and Magnolia's feet.

She shouted to warn the others: "Bear! Bear!" The two words were all she could manage.

A thorny bush caught at her skirt, pulling her back. She dove to the side, just as the bear crashed into it. She heard the rip of fabric as she wrenched herself away from the thorns and started running again.

The bear made a great swipe, and she felt the whoosh of its paw right behind her as she narrowly avoided another bush.

She swerved around a tree and found a log blocking her path.

Too high to jump.

She spun around. The bear had caught up and stood towering above her. Staring up at the beast, Trill caught her breath. It was huge.

Its mouth wrinkled as it snarled loudly at her.

Shutting her eyes tight, she pressed herself back against the rough bark.

Then she felt a surge of magic sweep past her, wrapping itself around the bear's head.

She hadn't done that.

She opened her eyes. The bear was slashing wildly at the air directly in front of its face.

She dodged around the distracted bear and ran a few steps, then pulled up short.

Eric sat on horseback in the middle of the bushes, with two of the knights who had come on the hunt. Magnolia sat behind one of the knights, hiding her face in his back. The three men were looking at the bear with shocked expressions.

Then Eric's eyes met hers, and he quickly turned his horse.

"Trill, get on."

She obliged, rushing forward to grab his hand. She almost pulled back, though, as their hands met and she felt a sharp zing of magic run through her.

It was him. He'd cast the spell.

He pulled her up behind him and lifted the reins. The horse turned sharply, and they burst into a gallop away from the bear, which seemed to be recovering from its confusion.

One of the knights blew a horn, and other horns responded in the distance. A few minutes later they passed the clearing where the hunting party had planned to meet for a mid-afternoon meal.

An uncontrollable light-headedness came over Trill, and she giggled.

"Bother," she said. "Now we've missed lunch."

Eric's shoulders gave a twitch, but he remained silent.

❧ 18 ❧

Christopher

Terrin pushed open the cloth doorway, stepping through first and holding it open for Chris and Thomas to follow. As the door fell shut behind him, Chris blinked rapidly to adjust to the barely lit room. Before he could make out more than dark shapes, he heard a cry of, "You found him!" and boots hitting the floor. Then someone was lifting him in a massive hug.

"Stop, Arnold! You'll hurt yourself." That was Nora's voice.

Chris dropped back to the floor. Now he could make out Arnold backing away, his face split ear to ear with a giant smile. Nora sat in a chair next to a swaying hammock, where he supposed Arnold had been sitting. Her eyes were round with amazement, but she had tilted her head so that her long hair hid most of her face.

"Arnold. Nora." Chris spoke slowly, rubbing the palm of his hand against his pant-leg.

At least no one else had punched him. Yet.

"How did you find him, Terrin?" asked Arnold.

"In mortal danger."

"And I missed it? Pity." If possible, he grinned more. But then the smile faded a bit. "Who's the friend?"

"This is Thomas," Chris said. "Thomas, this is Arnold and Nora."

As the three exchanged greetings, Chris stammered his apology to Nora and Arnold. His eyes dropped a bit, and he froze.

"Arnold, your hand."

Arnold glanced at his stump.

"This? It's nothing. Ran into some wolves coming down the mountain. Bit of a bite. Got infected, that's all."

"That's all? You lost your hand?"

"Bites fester quickly," said Thomas. "He could have lost his whole forearm."

Nora and Arnold both looked at Thomas, and Chris quickly explained. "Thomas is a healer."

"Was," Thomas amended for him.

Arnold opened his mouth, but Terrin cut in.

"So, Chris, could you read the stone?"

"You found it?" Chris said, somewhat surprised. He would have thought the cave nigh impossible to find. Then again, how else would they have known he was headed into the forest? They must have followed his trail.

"It looked like complete and utter gibberish," said Arnold. He was settling back down to the hammock with his stump across his lap.

"Thomas couldn't read it either."

"So what did it say?" Arnold leaned forward.

Chris took a deep breath, and then spoke. He had no trouble drawing the words from his memory. Besides reciting them ten times a day, they seemed stuck in his head like glue.

"Ho ho he he ha ha ho ho.
Twiddle your thumbs and dance.
Winter winds freeze away.
And sun doth rain its golden heat.
And I will laugh all day with
Ho ho he he ha ha ho ho,
And I will laugh all day!"

જી

Arnold

Arnold had to blink twice when he heard the riddle. He started to lean back against the wall, but the ridiculous hammock swayed beneath him, and he quickly leaned forward again.

Terrin had moved to the side of the room and was staring forward, frowning. Now she gave a slight nod.

"It's part of a song," she said.

Arnold raised his eyebrows. It wasn't part of any song he knew. He would remember a song with a verse like that. It sounded like whoever wrote it was drunk or delusional.

"What song?" Chris asked.

"One by the swamp people."

Oh, he thought. *Yep, delusional.*

"Do you think… Do you think we have to go to the swamp?" Nora's voice was quiet and hesitant.

Arnold agreed with her unspoken sentiment. The swamp was one of the most mysterious places in North Raec. It was almost impossible to navigate—take one wrong step, down you go, and nobody will ever find your body. And the swamp people were not known to appreciate trespassers.

Chris looked around at the group, meeting each of their eyes in turn. Then he slowly nodded.

"I suppose so. Do any of us know the way?"

Everyone looked at Terrin. She had always been the best at geography, and she had grown up in this forest, which shared a border with the swamp.

She nodded.

"Getting there is easy," she said. "Just go south. But I don't think anyone really knows their way around the swamp besides the swamp people."

But she didn't look as confident as she sounded. She leaned back against the wall, her chin dropping to her chest as her brow wrinkled with doubt.

"The only thing is," said Nora quietly, "Arnold probably shouldn't travel for a couple more weeks. Just to be safe."

Chris nodded.

"Right, then," he said. "We'll stay here until we're sure Arnold is up for the journey."

Arnold couldn't help harrumphing a little.

ॐ 19 ॐ

Terrin

Even with one hand gone, Arnold easily avoided or blocked Nora's attacks, their wooden practice swords making a rhythmic thwack-thwacking sound, dancing around the clearing. Terrin sat up a hill from them, back against a tree, only half watching as she soaked in the warm sun. She heard a slight rustle behind her tree, and she turned to look, expecting Chris or Dyani. Instead a man, only a few years older than her, came around and plopped down beside her.

Trunnen looked the same as ever.

"Terrin," he said, giving her a warm smile.

"Brother," she replied, returning the smile. "Why are you here?"

"Couple reasons. I see your friends are going at it."

She glanced down at where Nora and Arnold were still dueling.

"How do you know they're my friends?"

"Why else would they be here? Plainsmen aren't exactly common sight in the forest."

"True."

She leaned back against the tree, enjoying the feeling of rough bark.

"He's teaching her to fight," she said. "The world's a dangerous place, after all."

Trunnen did not reply for a moment, his head slightly bent as he watched the combat. Terrin also didn't feel the need to speak and tilted her own head back, allowing herself to almost doze.

"She must not be a very good student."

Terrin sat back up.

"What do you mean?"

"He's leaving plenty of openings, but she's only taken some of the most obvious."

She turned her full attention to the fight. Sure enough, Nora was not taking any sort of serious offensive. For a moment, Terrin was confused. Nora had shown herself to be quite competent with a sword.

Then she laughed.

Trunnen glanced at her, both eyebrows raised.

"Nora's more of a healer than a fighter. She's probably worried about over-extending him." She chuckled again. "When Arnold realizes, he's going to have a fit."

Trunnen gave a half smile but didn't laugh.

"Plains people are strange."

Shrugging, she changed the subject. "I'm assuming you didn't travel all day just to criticize my friends' sword lessons."

He reached into his pocket, and pulled out a small loop of string. At the end of it was a wood carving. He held it out to her.

"To remember us by, while you're gone."

She swallowed.

"It won't be that long," she said. "I won't forget you."

"A lot can happen in a year," he said.

Then he took her right hand and set the carving in her palm. She closed her fingers around it and glanced up at him.

After Chris and Nora decided to stay in the village for a while, Dyani had pestered Terrin into going to see her family in the neighboring village. They weren't expecting her home until summer, after graduation. She explained that she was traveling with some friends from the city, that they wanted to explore the world a little before settling down. She'd also told them she'd be back, hopefully within a year.

She hadn't mentioned that the moment anyone found out who Chris was, she'd be banished, too. Or else locked up for life, or worse.

She didn't tell them she was going to the swamp on the basis of a nonsense riddle.

Or that she hadn't actually graduated from school.

"What's wrong?" Trunnen leaned towards her, brow creased.

"It's just that you're right." She forced a smile. "A lot can change in a year."

He smiled and wrapped his arm around her. She leaned against his side, enjoying the warmth of his company.

She opened her palm and examined the carving. It was a fox, curled up. Its long, fluffy tail covered half its face, the tip flicking up just enough for its nose and one eye to peek out. Its ears were pressed flat. She gently lifted the string, sliding her wrist through the loop.

"Not half bad," she said, catching it in her fingers and rubbing her thumb against its back.

"You know I'm the best carver in Xell."

"Of course you are. But you know that's only because I didn't take the time to learn."

Trunnen shifted his arm enough to bat at the side of her head, but she blocked it with her own free arm. As she turned her head, she realized the thwack-thwacking had stopped. Nora had paused to get a drink.

Then Terrin caught Arnold's curious face looking up at her. Instinctively, she pulled away from Trunnen, escaping his hold as easily as a snake.

"Terrin?" he asked, following her to a standing position. "Are you sure you're all right?"

"Yes," she said quickly. Then she paused to take a breath before repeating slowly, "Yes, I'm fine."

She could tell that Trunnen was worried about her, but she couldn't explain everything that was going on.

Luckily, he didn't pursue the subject. He nodded briefly at the plainsmen.

"Come on then," he said. "I haven't given my greetings to Dyani yet."

With long strides, he disappeared down the trail to the village.

Terrin waved to her friends and turned to jog after him.

As soon as she came under the shadow of the trees, Terrin once again caught a glimpse of movement—someone's eyes in the underbrush. Only these eyes were a dark, muddy gray, surrounded by wrinkled gray skin and mud-coated hair.

Her stride faltered. But as quickly as before, the swamp-woman's face was gone.

"Keep up, Terrin!" Trunnen called.

"I must be going crazy," she muttered to herself before breaking into a flat-out run to catch her brother.

$\backsim$ 20 $\backsim$

Trillory

Good, he's alone, Trill thought as Eric stepped out of the hedge garden. Overhead, clouds were gathering, and the garden seemed almost gloomy in the gray, late-afternoon light. She left her seat on the wooden bench and hurried after him.

"Eric," she called, waving as he turned.

She had not been alone with him for more than a minute since the hunt. And even when she could have talked to him, she'd been afraid to mention the magic. She fell into step beside him. They walked in silence, and she swallowed hard.

Steeling herself, she spoke. "I… I haven't thanked you for the other day."

"What for?"

"You confused the bear. You used magic."

She glanced at him. It was possible she was wrong, perhaps he had a charm that he'd used. But it hadn't felt that way.

"Oh. You could sense that?" His fists clenched.

"Yes, I'm— Yes."

A small voice said in the back of her head, *If you're going to make him tell you, you should tell him.* But she hushed it. If their friendship ended here, if he was angry because she had found out about him, she couldn't let him know about her. He might tell his father, who would undoubtedly tell her own.

He sighed, and stared thoughtfully down the path. They had stopped by a bush of three-petaled orange flowers. Eric plucked one and rolled its stem in his hand for a bit, then shrugged.

"Come on. It'd be easiest to show you," he said.

He led her back to the castle. Trill couldn't say she regretted leaving the gardens. The air felt thick, and she guessed they were in for one last rain before summer. They went up through the castle, but she was surprised when they turned off into the north wing.

As he passed a servant, he paused and whispered something. The maid nodded and left.

They walked through the area she had explored, turned a corner, and stopped in front of a door. Eric pulled out a key.

"Is this why you chased me away the other day, when I was exploring?" Trill asked.

"Yeah. But it's not much, really."

The door clicked open, and they entered.

This room was different from all the others in the wing. There was no bed. Instead a table stood near the window, strewn with books. In one corner, a stone statue reminded her of the wooden practice dummies her brothers had used for swordplay. But mostly there were books. The wall beyond the table was entirely taken up by a bookshelf, crammed full. More books were stacked on the floor, with papers scattered about.

Eric looked around and grimaced.

"The servants can't get in except when I'm here," he said, "so the cleaning is mostly left to me, and ah…"

Trill suppressed a chuckle. What would a duke's son know about cleaning?

"But, why all the books?" she asked. "Surely they'd be better off in the library?"

Actually, she thought, these books might almost double the size of Duke Grith's library—and that was larger than most private collections she had seen.

"No, these are all mine. Well, they're my father's, but he gives them to me to study. Here, let me clear some space."

He set his flower on the table, then grabbed a broom and started pushing the books off to the side.

Trill picked up a volume, then gasped. It was no wonder these weren't in the library. The slightly cracked golden title made her almost want to drop the book.

The Magic Defense: Beginner Spells was not exactly standard reading.

Eric began to snatch it, then stopped.

"Sorry, I'm not used to letting people see them. Another reason the servants don't do the cleaning. We don't want too many to know. They might gossip and all."

"We. So your father's a magician, too?"

Eric nodded slowly.

"He's been teaching me, but I'm not very good. Father's touchy about it. He insists that I don't tell anyone. But since you found out anyway, I thought I could trust you."

He paused, his brow creased.

"I can, right?"

"I won't tell anyone," she said. "The people I spend most of my time with would probably laugh at me."

"You won't even tell Father, will you? He'd be mad that

I slipped up."

Trill nodded, and Eric smiled again.

"I'm glad someone else knows," he said. "I can't talk about it properly with Father. He always quizzes me. And even though you probably wouldn't find most of the theory and stuff that interesting, I do enjoy talking to you."

You should tell him, whispered the voice again.

But they were interrupted by a short knock on the door. The servant had brought a tray with a pitcher of water and several tiny sandwiches.

"I've always been curious about magic," Trill said, after the girl had gone. "My father never wanted anyone in his family to study it. Chris got in trouble once for bringing home a book on magic history from the school library."

She stopped, and clenched her jaw.

Eric didn't comment, but she had a feeling that he understood.

"Here," he said. "Let me show you something."

He shut the door, then gestured for her to sit down. Then, taking one more look at the flower, he touched her dress.

It was a plain dress, the most comfortable one she owned—a pale, gray cotton, no ruffles, with a white undershirt that showed at the neck. She had often worn it for casual garden work, and the gray had faded over the years.

She could feel the magic going out from his hand in a wave. She stared as, beginning at the sleeve where he'd touched it, a pale orange that matched the flower spread to cover the entire dress.

The tingly feeling faded, and then she felt it starting again. This time, the magic added a pattern of deeper orange leaves and flowers. He creased his brow, and a third wave of magic turned the undershirt to a warm cream.

He pulled away, but a nearly unnoticeable shell of magic

remained, slowly soaking into the fabric. He handed her the flower, which now matched her dress perfectly.

As Trill accepted the flower, she struggled to keep her voice calm.

"I see you have an eye for color," she said.

She tucked the flower gently into her hair.

He grinned.

"Orange suits you."

ॐ 21 ॐ

Arnold

Arnold checked his bag one last time. Nora had offered to help him pack, but he'd refused. Satisfied that everything was in place, he grabbed the strap and slung it over his shoulder.

Boots, jacket? All set.

Sword? Belts had been a struggle at first, when even bumping his stump caused it pain. But he'd figured out how to hold the strap so he could get the loose end through the buckle, and then it was mostly a matter of finagling until it was tight enough. He tugged again to make sure the belt and sword were secure. His weapons teacher had pounded in a certain measure of paranoia.

He swept the room with his eyes.

After the healer was satisfied they had gotten all the infection, he had moved from the medicine hut to a back room at Dyani's house. As wife of the village chief, she had one of the few homes large enough to host visitors. Unfortunately, there had been more hanging cots—he was glad to finally be leaving those behind.

He exited the room and started around the back of the house.

"Took you long enough," Terrin said, meeting him halfway around. "You should have at least let Chris help you."

"I got it," Arnold said.

Chris and Thomas had shared the room with him, but the packing that took him ten minutes, they finished in two.

As he and Terrin came around the back of the house to the small lean-to stable, he was annoyed—though not surprised—to see Rich was already saddled. He had not yet had a chance to attempt saddling.

He fastened his bag behind his saddle, then mounted. He had to go around to the other side, so he could grab the pommel in his right hand. It was something he'd practiced many times before, but it felt different now that he was doing it from necessity.

The others also mounted.

"Farewell, Dyani of Xell. We thank you, and your village, for your hospitality," Chris said, inclining his head towards Dyani. "May we one day return the favor."

She smiled and nodded in return.

"Farewell, Christopher, Thomas, and Arnold of plains, Nora of Yorc, and Terrin of Xell. May your travels be profitable. I will remember your offer."

She paused, then continued in a less formal tone. "Take care of yourselves."

"Thank you," said Chris.

He nudged Marc forward.

"Don't worry," Arnold said, suddenly grinning. "We obviously do a great job of that." He waved with his left arm.

He could sense Terrin rolling her eyes, but Dyani smiled.

"Don't lose that attitude, Arnold," she said, waving back. "It suits you well."

It felt good to finally be on the road again. The month they had spent in the village since Chris's return had felt more akin to forever. Arnold had vented some of his energy by teaching Nora, but still he'd been restless.

Chris, though he tried to hide it, had been even more so. The forest people's loyalty to the crown was famous. Very few would have hesitated to turn him in if they'd known he was banished. Still, he had seemed to enjoy talking with Dyani and her husband. They couldn't tell him much about King Miles, since the forest people cared little for history, but they were wise in other lore.

Of course Nora hadn't minded the wait. She'd spent most of her time with healer Koresh, learning of forest herbs. Arnold and Nora quickly discovered that a simple question could keep him talking for what felt like hours, and Nora had the patience to listen.

While Arnold had not the fortitude for Koresh, in Thomas he'd found a mixture of humor and wisdom. The old man had disappeared for about a week, collecting herbs in the forest. Once he returned, though, Thomas had shown Arnold several exercises for regaining strength and cheered him with anecdotes of his past patients. He even proved to have some skill with a sword and assisted with Nora's lessons.

Then there was Terrin. He glanced across at the tall girl. Her straight, brown hair fell over her shoulders, her sharp features pointed up towards the sky. She, unlike Chris, had long ago mastered the art of hiding her emotions. But he'd seen her the other day with her brother. Even before that, he'd seen how relaxed she was in her forest. Relaxed in a way he'd never seen her before.

Regardless, they were leaving now. Within a few days, they expected to reach a small stable where they could leave the horses. Then sometime the following day, they would reach the swamp.

From there, they would have to improvise.

❧ 22 ❧

Nora

The cold water felt good as it ran down Nora's throat. Sword lessons were tiring, but fun. Not to mention, they made everything taste better. She savored the last drops, then set down the now-empty clay cup.

"Thank you," she said to the forest man.

He nodded back.

This was one of four stopping posts for anyone coming and going from the swamp. Horses could not traverse the muck, so about a hundred years ago the king set up stables for the sake of travelers like themselves. Not that there were many. Chris had been reluctant to show his face here, but as Thomas pointed out, if no one recognized him in their month at the village, one day here would not matter.

Nora climbed up to the loft and started to lay out her bedding for the night. Terrin was already asleep. As was Arnold, who had gone straight to bed after the day's lesson. Her eyes settled on Chris's empty spot. Her hand paused against her bag.

The entire month since he had returned, she had barely spoken to him. Only earlier that day, Terrin had chided her for it.

"He's not going to leave again," she had said. "And it's not your fault he left the first time."

Nora turned and opened her bag, pulling out a much smaller, older bag. It was made of supple leather that felt cool to the touch. Out of habit she ran her fingers along the cracking paint. The bag had been passed down through her mother's family for who knew how long. Her aunt had given it to her before she'd left for school the first time. Since then she had stored her most precious possessions in it.

There weren't many, and she quickly found the wooden flute she was searching for. It wasn't really a flute, too short and simple. But there was no better name for it.

Now, to find Chris.

❧

Christopher

Chris ran the cloth over Marc one last time, and stepped back to admire his handiwork. The horse still looked more grayish-brown than white. Marc looked at him and nickered, the other horses echoed the sound.

"What?" Chris said, just as a sharp tweet sounded in his ear. He jumped and turned, but it was only Nora, holding a wooden tube.

She extended it to him, and he took it. She went to visit her own horse.

He examined the tube.

It's some sort of flute, he thought as he ran his fingers over the few holes, and around the mouthpiece. There was a small crack on either side, finer than a strand of hair, which told him it had once been two pieces.

"It looks well made," he said.

"Good. I made it myself," Nora said.

She turned to face him, and Minty head-butted her. She laughed and turned halfway back to continue patting the horse.

"I didn't know you carved," Chris said.

She shrugged and leaned into the horse, gazing out of the stables and into the shadows beyond.

Chris looked at her. She had so many skills he had never expected from her.

"Play it," Nora said suddenly, glancing at him. Her eyes shone.

Chris obediently lifted it to his mouth and tested each note. Then he tried a short song. He'd once thought about becoming a minstrel, but had quickly given up that dream—his father would have been horrified.

"You play it almost as well as me," she said.

"Nonsense. I'm sure I can play better than you. That tune was just a test."

"You might be skilled with stringed instruments, but we mountain folk are natural pipers."

"Well, then, you play it," he said, offering it back.

"No, it's yours. Think of it as a welcome-back gift."

"Oh," he said, and he dropped his hand, his fingers folding around the instrument.

"You should join me and Arnold at swordplay," she said. "It was your idea in the first place."

Chris faked a groan. "If I do that, Arnold will make me duel him."

"You two used to duel all the time, and you loved it."

"Back when I could beat him, yeah. Now he's a real knight."

"Terrin still wins almost every time."

"He lets her."

Nora smirked, and cocked her head.

"How do you know that he didn't let you win, before?" she asked.

"Nonsense," Chris said, though he'd wondered the same thing. "It's one thing to let a girl beat you when you're grown, quite another to let a man beat you when you're young."

"Are you calling Terrin a *girl?*" Nora asked, raising her eyebrows. A barely contained smile quirked the edge of her mouth.

"Irrelevant," Chris huffed.

"Well, I remember once, when you were fifteen, and he dropped his guard wide open for you, right when you were ready to strike."

"How would you remember something like that?" Chris laughed. "In fact, I'm positive you're making it up."

"Why don't you ask him?"

"Because he certainly wouldn't remember."

"Uh, huuuh," she said. "Keep telling yourself that."

They both laughed longer than the joke deserved, enjoying the release of a month's worth of tension.

When they recovered, Nora spoke first. "But seriously, I'm tired of losing all the time. I have to take Arnold's word for it that I'm actually improving."

"Are you saying you could beat me?"

"Oh, don't start that," Nora said.

The horses nickered, as if in agreement.

"All right, I won't. But I am curious," he said as he put away his grooming equipment.

It wasn't till he was done that Nora finally said, "No. No, I can't even beat Thomas, without some luck. I couldn't beat you now."

For a second he thought about teasing her on the last word, but he decided against it. It was getting late, he was tired, and tomorrow they would enter the swamp.

❦ 23 ❦

Terrin

The long wooden raft skimmed along the water, then bumped gently to a stop against a dirt bar. Terrin waited for the swamp girl to tie off, and then the four of them trooped out: a tall man with sandy hair, a stocky youth, the swamp girl, and Terrin.

"That is a *big* tree," said the stocky boy. Before them was a tree so wide that the four of them together wouldn't be able to reach halfway around. Its huge trunk rose to the canopy above, where it disappeared from sight. In the front was a large, ornately carved door.

But Terrin's gaze had slipped to the side, just beyond the tree. On another, larger isle she saw a great black head, sticking out of the small bushes that grew there.

She stifled a squeak, then a giggle. It was just a wraith, and it did not look anything more than curious.

Strange, she thought. *I always considered wraiths forest animals.*

"It has never opened," said the swamp girl, calling Terrin's attention back to the door in the tree.

The tall man approached it. He rubbed his hands along the carvings.

Terrin glanced beyond the tree once again, back to the wraith. This time she nearly choked on her subdued yell. Beside the wraith stood an old woman, eyes trained on the swamp girl, with a frown that creased her entire face. The wraith bumped its head against the woman's hand, and the woman patted it. Then they retreated into the brush.

"You okay, Roz?"

Terrin jerked her attention back to the others. The tall man was looking the direction she had been. He turned back to her and half frowned, half smiled.

Behind him the door had split down the middle and was standing open. The stocky young man leaned against it, grinning smugly, while the swamp girl gaped.

"There's nothing there," the tall man said, still watching her. "Were you dreaming again?"

❧

Terrin gasped and sat up. She took several deep breaths, blinking sleepiness from her eyes. A film of water covered her face, and she thought for a moment she was sweating. Then she realized that a blanket of mist covered the whole camp, rising from the swamp water all around.

A few feet away, Nora was trying to coax a small fire back to life.

Terrin rose and stretched. She wished she could walk around to work the kinks out of her muscles, but the dirt bar was cramped, barely supporting the five people and their gear.

A flame flickered to life, and Nora whooped.

The other three sleepers jerked upright.

"Where's the dragon?" said Arnold.

Terrin laughed. Then she shook out her hair, brushing back the strands that fell in front of her face. She crouched and straightened her blankets to roll them up.

Something prickled at the base of her neck. She froze, afraid for a second that it was magic. But no, this was a different tingle, the type she got when she was missing something—or was being watched. She turned her head, searching the surrounding isles. Her eyes moved quickly from bush to bush, but she saw nothing.

She sighed, rubbing the grit from the corners of her eyes. She was getting paranoid.

Or whoever was watching them was well hidden.

She returned to packing. The smell of cooking meat made her mouth water.

"I'm going to feel out our path from here," said Chris.

He splashed away into the swamp before the others could acknowledge his words.

Terrin watched him go. Her thoughts returned to her dream. Should she tell him?

She glanced up, as if expecting the giant tree to appear. But while they were surrounded by many large trees, none were that big. Then again, it wasn't really the tree that bothered her, it was the people. The dream had been from someone else's perspective, which was strange. It had been so vivid—she hadn't realized she wasn't in control till the man called her 'Roz.'

Terrin watched Chris plunge a stick into the water, maybe a hundred feet away.

No, she couldn't. She hated the idea of trusting magical dreams to lead them. She would wait for proof of the tree's existence—and maybe its importance—before encouraging Chris on his wild goose chase.

Or maybe you're just afraid, said a tiny voice in her head.

I'm not! Terrin snapped back, almost speaking the words out loud. She licked her lips and took a breath.

Of course I don't like the idea of magic worming its way into my head and taking over my dreams, she told herself. *But I'm not afraid of a stupid tree.*

Then there was the other obvious question: the old woman Roz had seen—would see? She bore a striking resemblance to Terrin's own mysterious old lady. The dream woman was perhaps a bit younger, and her hair more silver than gray, but Terrin couldn't help wondering if the magic had been working in her mind all along, causing her to imagine things in the real world.

"Breakfast is done," Nora called.

"'Bout time," said Arnold. "I was going to starve between boredom and hunger."

He plopped himself down beside Terrin.

"You can't starve of boredom," she said.

"That's what you say."

Nora began to place the long strips of meat onto slices of bread.

"This will have to do for plates," she said, handing the first one to Thomas. "I'm not going to wash any di— Chris! You'll get muck all over your clothes."

Terrin turned and saw that Chris had returned, his boots coated in mud.

"I'll just have to be careful," he said, sitting down. A streak of mud smeared his pant leg.

Nora, however, did not notice as she turned to hand Terrin her breakfast. Terrin nodded thanks and then took a bite, scanning the swamp.

There, less than fifty feet away, was a pale girl with long brown hair, covered in gray mud.

❧ 24 ❧

Nora

Terrin exhaled sharply, creating a hissing sound. Nora looked up. Terrin jerked at Chris's sleeve and nodded to a clump of bushes several islands away.

And to the skinny girl that was crouched there.

The girl didn't seem to mind being seen. She stared back. A frown was etched in her face, and—though Nora couldn't be sure—she thought that the girl's eyes were focused on Terrin.

"Hello, there," Chris called.

The girl glanced at him, then disappeared with a swish of her hair.

They sat in silence for a while. Nora, at least, felt slightly in shock.

"Good to know we're not being watched, or anything," said Arnold.

Terrin and Chris shook their heads.

"No, this is good," he said. "It's swamp custom for visitors to be watched. Unless they decide we're a threat, they shouldn't harm us. And if they decide to trust us, they might even guide us to where we need to go."

And where's that? Nora wondered.

"Oh. Then what could go wrong?" Arnold said lightly, though his smile was weak. "There's obviously nothing threatening about us."

☙

The tuft of brown grass squished under Nora's feet. She winced as one foot slid forward several inches beyond where she intended to step. The ground had been getting steadily wetter since they entered the swamp. The trees around them had, at first, been mostly on dry ground, but now each trunk sank a few feet under water.

Why would someone want to live here? The trees looked stunning in the half-light created by their canopies, but every step made her feel like she might sink into the murky waters.

"I'm never going to get these boots cleaned," muttered Arnold behind her. Then louder, "Chris, if we don't find this next riddle or whatever here, you're buying me new boots—"

Chris chuckled.

"—In fact, I think you should buy me new boots anyway."

"Nonsense." Terrin shook her head. "Cleaning them will build character. After all, a knight should always clean his own boots, no matter how hard it is. Unless he has a squire, of course."

"Drat. I knew I should have accepted that crazy kid's offer."

"Maybe you should have," she responded. "He would have at least matched you in brain power."

Nora laughed, nearly losing her balance as her foot splashed into cold water instead of mud. Knights were not permitted to have a squire in their first year, or until they had earned their own coat of arms. Arnold had been made a knight barely two weeks before Chris was banished, and he certainly didn't have arms. For someone to have asked to be his squire—Nora had to hold still for a bit to let the laughter pass.

They trudged up a hill that rose out of the water like a small isle. Nora paused to enjoy the firmer ground. Arnold and Terrin slogged past, but Thomas stopped to talk with her.

"You know, swamps might be muddy, but there are many herbs that don't grow anywhere else in North Raec. Like moon's-honey."

"What's that?" Nora asked, smiling.

Thomas enjoyed sharing information in a way that would have made him a great teacher, and she had an equal interest in learning.

"For one thing, it does wonders for burns, but mostly it cures magical wounds."

"Magical wounds?"

"Yes, it increases one's resistance to magic. Of course, it can't undo what the magic has already done, but it keeps it from worsening. I've never actually had need of it, magicians being so rare any more. But one can never be too prepared—especially healers.

"The flower's easy enough to recognize. Its petals are white. Normally it's closed up in a bulb, but under moonlight they spread out." He illustrated with his hands. "Thus the name."

"How do you use it?"

"That depends on the type of magic. For a physical injury or burn, you use the leaves to make a paste, which you then apply to the wound. It sucks the magic right out. Normally one coat will do the job, but if it doesn't, then you apply a new coat once an hour."

Nora nodded.

"However, there are spells that affect one's mind. For those, you have to find the flower in moonlight and collect its pollen. Fix it as tea, and it'll cure most any magical ailment. It's a rare herb, though, quite hard to gather, and there's also the danger that if overused it will cause sickness, even resulting in death. And if a magician were to drink it… well, it's quite possible they'd lose use of their magic."

"Permanently?" asked Nora, frowning.

"I don't know for sure," he said, thoughtfully tapping his chin. "The pollen absorbs magic, so I think once the pollen had moved through the system, the magic could return in time. There are a couple of herbs that might speed the process. However, I'm afraid it's quite untested."

"Then how do you tell for sure if your patient needs the pollen? And what if they don't know whether they are magicians?" pressed Nora.

"That is the interesting, and hard to answer, question. Since, outside of magicians, people can only sense magic that is either very powerful, or used on themselves, it is largely left to the patient's discretion. But there are a few signs, such as…"

The conversation continued for several minutes. Then the ground thinned out, and they had to walk single file.

It wasn't till Nora nearly slipped again that she realized how effectively the lesson had distracted her from her displeasure with the swamp. Too bad it couldn't have continued.

ᛒ

Arnold

As the light began to fade, they set up camp on the biggest isle they could find. Even so, there was not much room to lay out their bedding. Bushes were rampant on any isle that could support them. This also meant that Arnold couldn't practice sword-play. He'd been working with Nora daily for a month, and though marching through the swamp was definitely exercise, it was not nearly as satisfying.

Just as well he had the first watch. He felt wide awake. Knowing that someone was spying on them didn't help, either.

Then Nora settled beside him, lowering herself carefully to the ground.

"Not tired?" he asked.

"Something like that," she said. She pulled her knees up to her chest, wrapping her arms around them, and stifled a yawn. "But more like so tired I can't sleep. Never thought I'd experience that."

"I know that feeling," he said.

"As I recall, you and Chris used to get into quite a bit of trouble when you had that feeling," said Nora.

When they were children, Chris had requested that he and Arnold stay in the school dormitories. While there, Arnold had taken him, and occasionally Terrin, on many night escapades, often to the kitchen. Eventually, the earl grew fed up with their behavior and had them return to his manor.

This was surely what Nora was referring to, but he faked a hurt expression—though in the dusky light he wasn't sure it had any effect—and said, "I don't know what you're talking about."

"I'm sure you don't."

"Besides, most of that happened before you got to school, so how would you even know?"

"Well, I'm pretty sure that counts as a confession. But Terrin told me all sorts of stories of your 'adventures.'"

She yawned.

They sat in silence for a while, and Arnold wondered if she'd fallen asleep.

Then there was a loud creak.

They both jumped, and their eyes searched the swamp. But the sound did not repeat.

Nora drew her legs tighter, her face looking nearly as pale as the swamp girl's in the poor light. For the next hour or so that she sat with him, she did not yawn again.

ശ 25 ശ

Trillory

"Fire, come, and light. Surge, burn, turn my foes to ash," muttered Eric.

Between his palms, Trill could see a small spark of flame. It showed no interest in his words.

She sensed the tendrils of magic that spilled from his fingers and reached towards the flame. A few strands had twisted themselves into a ball around it, but the rest either scattered before they reach the ball, or surged past without attaching.

Eric said the words were supposed to help guide the magic, but they didn't seem to be helping him much.

She turned back to her reading. Manipulative spells. She had thought she might find the confusion spell here, but the book had no index. This probably wouldn't have been a problem—she didn't really want to learn magic—but she was curious about the bear. For one thing, the form of the magic had felt familiar. It had reminded her of the night of the ball.

The night Chris had been framed.

Every spell seemed to have its own set of rules. She noticed one that would cause a person to 'decide' to hold still, but the spell would break if the person's life was threatened. There also seemed to be dozens of variations on the same spell. For instance, one spell took such complete control that the person wouldn't do anything without orders, while another left them relatively free but allowed you to influence their actions.

One thing was consistent, though. All the spells limited what other magic the caster could use.

But despite the restrictions, Trill couldn't help worrying what would happen if someone like Anthony got a hold of these spells. If he had magic, his cruel streak could do serious damage.

She also understood now why her father made his family wear charms to protect against such spells. But it made her wonder why more courtiers didn't use them. The only other person she'd sensed that sort of charm magic around was Crown Prince Tyler.

Even though magicians were rare, why would anyone take the chance?

Trill poured herself a fresh cup of water and glanced at Eric. He had succeeded in guiding more magic to the ball, and his spark had grown to the size of a teacup. She smiled.

She'd spent most of her time the last few weeks in this room. She found Eric was easygoing and friendly, a nice change from Joline. At first she'd also used the room to avoid Anthony, but a couple weeks ago he had mysteriously left on 'business.' It irked her—if their father had known Anthony would be gone, perhaps he would have let her come home—but she did not mind so much as she would have before Eric befriended her.

The dry pages of the book rustled as she flipped to the next page. This spell made someone agree with everything you say, and answer yes to all your questions. Her eyes went past the incantation to the notes.

This spell will not work if the subject has eaten pancakes for breakfast, Trill began to read. *Also, in the event of—*

Trill stopped and reread the first sentence.

Pancakes?

She couldn't stop the laughter that surged from her chest.

She dropped the book and tried to smother the sound, but already she sensed Eric's magic faltering. She looked up in time to see the fire fall from its place between his hands. The magic tendrils that had held it in place had snapped. The fire hit the floor and flattened.

Then it flickered and vanished.

Trill let out a long breath, and looked up to meet Eric's eyes.

"I'm sorry," she said.

"It's okay," he said, smiling a bit. "I was about to lose it anyway. What's so funny?"

He stepped toward her to examine the book.

"Well, it's just that I never realized that what someone ate for breakfast could affect magic," said Trill, showing him the spell.

He chuckled.

"Well, I knew there were certain herbs that affected magic, but that is strangely specific."

There was a scream from the doorway. Trill looked up to see a maid, her fingers white around a shaking tray of tea and cakes. The girl's eyes were locked on the floor.

Trill followed her gaze to where the fire had been.

To where the fire was.

Though the original flames had died out, a spark must have caught one of the many loose pages that littered the floor. Now the fire was surging back to life with more energy than ever.

Trill jumped to her feet as Eric turned towards the flame. She reached for the pitcher on the table, but her instincts were already taking over. The water surged from the pitcher, brushing across her extended hand.

Her other hand shifted, grasping the magic that had wrapped itself around the water, flinging it across the room without the slow grace that normally accompanied her magic. As the water touched the fire she opened her fingers so that it spread, covering the flames. Then she closed her hand into a fist so that the water closed around the flame, dousing it.

She stood there a second, then released the water and swayed into the table, grasping the edge with one hand. It wasn't that she was in any way exhausted by the magic—in fact, she felt slightly exhilarated—but that she was shocked at how automatically it had come.

So much for her secret.

"Here, Kelly, let me take that," she heard Eric say, "and you take this. And it would be best if you didn't mention this to anyone."

"Y-yes, m'lord."

Trill glanced up to see the maid clutch the now-empty pitcher to her chest. She dropped a quick curtsy and backed out of the room.

Eric set down the tray and picked up a towel that lay by the window. He dropped it across the pool of water. Without giving it more attention, he turned back to the table and poured two cups of tea. He handed one to her. After a careful drink from his cup, he sat down across from where Trill still stood.

Trill met his eyes, waiting for him to comment on her magic.

Instead he said, "Well, that could have gone worse."

Trill sat and took a shaky sip of her own tea.

"Maybe you shouldn't leave paper lying around when you're playing with fire," she said.

"Yes, well. I've never been great at the whole safety thing."

They stared at each other for a moment, and then Trill's eyes dropped to the table. Eric's fingers drummed against the wood, and she noticed that the table seemed to be rapidly changing colors, at first only slightly, and then becoming brighter and brighter.

Then the drumming stopped, and the table remained a florescent pink.

Trill glanced up at Eric and raised her eyebrows.

He grinned, and the table went back to normal.

"So, how long have you known about your powers?" he asked.

Trill blinked. "Er, what?"

"Well, at first I assumed you didn't know," he said. "But considering you're not in shock—"

"Wait, you knew?"

"Don't change the subject."

Trill set down her cup and leaned back. She crossed her arms, glaring at him.

"Well, you did make it kind of obvious," he said. "Aside from the forest people, I don't think anyone can sense magic unless it's very strong, or unless they themselves are magicians."

He waved toward the window. "What I cast at that bear was a very minor confusion spell—there was hardly any power in it. Since you could sense it, the obvious conclusion was that you were a magician. Now, my question."

Trill dropped her eyes.

She should have been more careful. After all, Chris had never sensed her magic, but she never thought about that.

Well, it was too late now.

"So? How long have you known?" Eric repeated.

"As long as I can remember."

"Really?" he said.

Trill looked up at the surprise in his voice.

"I could barely do anything before I was twelve," he said, "and what I managed was only because my father taught me. You must be powerful. Why didn't you tell anyone?"

Trill shrugged.

"At first, I didn't want to," she said. "It was fun to have a secret. And then later, I figured my father wouldn't approve. He… distrusts magic, to say the least. And besides, had he let me learn, I would have had to take lessons from the Shard's caretaker, and he is a stodgy old man."

"Well, how would you like to learn now?"

❧ 26 ❧

Brayden

There was a soft bump as the boat settled herself into the dock. A minute later she was tied off and the plank had been lowered. Travelers hurried down first, some going to the side so that they were nearby to oversee the unloading of their belongings. Brayden walked down the plank, trying to control his bounce. He'd waited till the first crowd had thinned, so as to lessen his risks of a clumsy accident.

There were so many reasons that North Raec should be proud of their sister country, not angry. Looking around, he was impressed by the buzz of merchants from all over the world. Colyth was a remarkable city, one of the top five trading centers of the world—though that report was from last year. It was also the capital of South Raec.

Which was good, because Brayden didn't want to travel much longer on his own. He had hardly trusted himself to keep track of his father's letter this long.

Someone roughly pushed into him from behind. He tumbled forward, and then quickly moved himself towards the side of the street, as the sailor who'd bumped him cursed and moved on. Brayden tightened his grip on the satchel he carried, and continued onward, towards the back of town.

At first he made himself hurry, but soon he was taken in by his surroundings. He had never traveled far from home, besides the short hunting trips, and though Coricstead had a fine market, it was nothing compared to the sweet smells that now tickled his nostrils and the bright colors that attracted his eyes.

"Finest clothes from Diamond Isles!" called a loud voice, obviously accented.

"Sweeter fruits here than anywhere," cried another.

So many people, all wanting to be heard over everyone else. It reminded him a bit of court life, all the nobles trying to draw the king's attention. He chuckled.

It took him an hour to slowly make his way through the crowds. He couldn't help but stop to listen to the street musicians or look at the exotic goods. He was constantly bumped, and eventually he moved his satchel forward where he could keep a better eye on it, and he was careful not to knock anyone over himself.

When he did reach the castle, he had to say it didn't match the rest of Colyth's bright colors. It was smaller than his father's castle, though the courtyard looked bigger. The gray walls rose high above the murky moat.

Taking a deep breath, he started across the drawbridge. He was met by a short servant, who looked to be only twelve. His small, round face was topped with a bowl of brown hair, and he was dressed in a red tunic and red leggings. He had a big grin as he met Brayden.

"Greetin's, sir. What be yer business?"

Brayden couldn't help but grin back at the boy's clipped speech, wondering if the servant always spoke like this or was doing it because he thought him a simpleton. No one could blame the boy for it. In his rugged traveling clothes, Brayden didn't look much like a diplomat.

"I have a message for the North Raecan ambassador, from King Nylan Coric."

The boy flushed a bit.

"Oh. I'm sorry, sir. I didn't mean to be rude. 'Cour— Of course, I'll take you right to him."

"'Tis fine," Brayden said, 'laxing his own grammar in an attempt to make the boy more comfortable.

With a quick bow, the boy led him across the courtyard. Brayden couldn't help wondering how the lad would have reacted if he knew he was talking to a prince.

"I'll take you to one of the lounges, and then go straight to fetch the ambassador, sir."

"Thank you."

Arnold

They were now walking almost constantly in ankle-deep water. It felt like for every step they took towards the center of the swamp, they took three in the opposite direction to avoid a section of too-soft ground. Absentmindedly, Arnold tried to rub his sleep-blurred eyes—Chris had gotten them moving first thing—but only a stump bumped his head. He winced at his forgetfulness and dropped the arm back to his side.

The stump wasn't sore anymore, but every time he had drawn his sword to practice, it had made him feel oddly off balance. And every once in a while, he would find himself trying to do something, like scratch his forehead, or brush back his bangs, or brush something off his clothes. And sometimes, like now, he would feel the intense need to scratch the palm of his now non-existent hand. He clenched his right hand into a fist, and pressed his left arm against his side.

He had told everyone that it was just a hand, that he was still fine. But even when he didn't need two hands—it only took one to hold a sword—he still felt completely useless.

"Here." Thomas said, startling Arnold. He was holding out a yellow leaf with sawed edges.

"What is it?" said Arnold, taking it gingerly. He wasn't sure if he trusted anything of that color—though on closer examination, the other side was a vibrant green.

"Put it in your mouth and suck on it for a while. It'll help with ghost itches. I had nearly forgotten it existed—not needed very often, outside of wars—but it grows thickly here in the swamp. Pick it, let it wilt a couple days, and then suck on it. I've been picking a few leaves here and there, and by the time we leave, I should have enough to last you a while."

When Arnold still hesitated, Thomas laughed. "It doesn't even taste too bad."

Arnold rubbed the leaf between his fingers. "I'm not sure I can trust a medicine that doesn't taste bad."

"Yes, most of us healers are of the same opinion. But I'm afraid that in this case, there's not much choice."

"I knew you healers did it on purpose."

He placed the herb on his tongue, and a mild sweetness flooded his mouth. A few seconds later the itching began to fade.

"I've heard that the swamp people use it to sweeten their water," the old man continued. "Some people say it purifies as well as sweetening, but who can tell?"

"Thank you, Thomas."

"Ah, don't thank me. I can't help it. And besides, imagine how dull things would be without your jokes."

They both smiled.

"Now, we'd better get back to walking," Thomas added.

Arnold looked up and realized that the others had pulled ahead by several yards, though they had paused to wait on an isle.

As the morning passed, Arnold noticed odd sounds—splashes that didn't sound quite like fish, an odd creak or snap. Occasionally he felt like eyes were staring into him. Whenever he searched for the source, he would see nothing. Sometimes he thought he saw a branch flip back into place, or ripples in the water. There was even once or twice when he thought he saw a flash of hair, or the features of a face, out of the corners of his eyes.

It was a bit past mid-morning when Chris called back, "Dead end."

They had reached a larger island, and the ground was surprisingly dry. As usual, it was crowded with bushes.

Arnold moved forward past Terrin, to see what Chris was looking at. This was not the first time the swamp had forced them to try another way, but this time the blockade was more extreme. The island ended in a two foot drop to an area of fast-flowing current nearly two yards across. On the other side, the bank of the next island rose even steeper.

"Well," said Arnold, as Nora and Thomas came up beside him, "it's not really a dead end. It's actually quite lively."

No one laughed, though Thomas and Nora smiled slightly, and he sighed. The swamp was a dreary, bug-infested place. Between the mugginess, the difficult footing, and being watched, they were all starting to wear out.

"Fine," said Chris, stepping away from the edge. Then he called, "If you're going to help us, then help us. We know you're there."

There was dead silence.

Then an eerie voice responded, "I am the second sentry of Shylak, and I hear your cry. But tell me, why did you enter our land?"

Arnold had always thought the swamp people a bit crazy—why else would they live in a swamp?—but the voice sent shivers up his spine.

"We wish to go to Shylak," responded Chris. "There is something we need your help with."

"What?"

"Our business is—hard to explain. I would speak to your elders about it."

"And what would you give us in return?"

The voice seemed to have dropped deeper, and Arnold wondered if it really belonged to the girl they had seen. And what would Chris do now? They didn't really have anything to give. Thomas had brought some gold, but—

"We bring the gift of friendship," declared Chris.

A second later, a wooden raft appeared to their left, from beyond an isle thick with vegetation, maybe twenty yards away. The same girl from earlier stood on it, guiding the craft with a long paddle as she pushed off the isle. She stood, holding her paddle still and letting the boat glide towards them. A slight smile was on her face as she spoke in a voice that was not eerie, but rather soft and sweet.

"The greatest gift that one can give."

❧ 28 ❧

Terrin

The wooden planks of the bridge creaked and swayed as the companions made their way across. Arnold was starting to look a bit green in the face, and Terrin wondered if his stump made balance more difficult. She dropped back to walk by him.

"Remember to breathe," she said.

He gave her a sour look, but then he took several deeper breaths.

"It's easier if you don't think about it," she added.

"How exactly does one do that? It's kinda hard not to think about the ground when it keeps bucking beneath your feet. This is worse than a hammock."

"Just relax."

"She's right," said Thomas, dropping back to walk beside them. "Sometimes our bodies do things better without the aid of our minds. The trick is to distract yourself. You might try focusing more on the scenery."

Terrin looked around. Shylak was a marvel of engineering. It sat near the center of the swamp, where the trees were largest. The city was built entirely above the water. The bulk of it consisted of wooden platforms, supported by branches and connected by broad, rope bridges like the one they were walking on. Many of the platforms also had rope ladders leading up higher, to buildings that nestled behind more branches. These were mostly connected in groups of two or three, sometimes reaching up to a third level that nearly disappeared into the canopy of leaves.

Though Shylak was not as active as Fredricburg, the presence of the locals was more pronounced. The 'streets' were just as crowded, if not more, and Terrin could feel the people's stares prickling her skin from every direction.

As they moved from the bridge to one of the platforms, she glanced over the edge. Below them, an occasional fish jumped from the water, snapping at insects. A few rafts coasted between the trees, carting various things like fish or brush.

"We're almost there. Two more platforms," said Ceianna.

Terrin glanced up, and for a moment she met the swamp girl's eyes.

Immediately Terrin jerked her eyes away. She strode to the tree at the center of the platform and rubbed her hands against the bark. The roughness under her fingers helped her focus.

Though the swamp people had always looked very similar to Terrin, there was something about Ceianna that was strikingly like the girl from her dream, the one who had guided Roz and her friends to the tree. When she had first spotted her, Terrin had thought they were one and the same. But on closer inspection, she could see that Ceianna had higher cheek bones, and her eyes were more gold than brown.

Nevertheless, it was unsettling.

Terrin pushed herself away from the tree and glanced back at

Arnold. He seemed more comfortable on the platforms, but he was still taking his time. He also kept clear of the edges, for which she didn't blame him—the wooden rail around the edge looked far too flimsy to support his weight.

However, he managed to cross the next bridge with more ease.

As they crossed the last bridge, Terrin examined their goal. The tree was the biggest they had seen so far. Though it was obviously dead, few of the thick branches had broken off. It had only a small platform, but an ornate door was set into the trunk.

A man leaned casually to the side of the door, watching as they approached.

They filed out onto the platform, and Ceianna nodded to the man. "Elder, these are Chris, Thomas, Arnold, Terrin, and Nora. They have come to us seeking assistance in return for friendship."

The man looked them over. Only at the word 'elder' did Terrin look close enough to realize that the man was quite old. The mud that the swamp people wore like a badge had disguised his gray hair and wrinkled skin, but what had fooled her even more was his straight back and easy stance. He seemed full of strength and energy.

He examined them each carefully before speaking.

"Welcome, friends. I hope your journey has not been too hard."

"And yours, elder," answered Chris, bowing a bit deeper than Ceianna had done.

The elder smiled. "You have studied our ways? Welcome, indeed. Not many take the time to learn about us swamp folk."

Terrin smiled, remembering how Chris had always enjoyed studying other cultures.

The elder continued, "But I can see you have journeyed long. It is not good to discuss business when tired. Go, explore our city, eat our food, and sleep here tonight. Tomorrow we shall talk.

"For now Ceianna, as second sentry, will be your guide."

He nodded briskly to them, then disappeared through the door before Terrin's thoughts could gather.

Ceianna turned to them.

"Very well, this way," she said, and gestured towards another bridge.

Arnold groaned.

Terrin turned to follow Ceianna, and something that had been bugging her finally clicked.

Ceianna was the second sentry of Shylak.

But if she was second, where was the first?

ↄ 29 ↄ

Terrin

Shylak's marketplace was set up where several trees grew so close that the platforms merged into one large plaza. It seemed to also double as a meeting place, for most of the swamp people were more interested in talking than in wares.

Of course, they could just be gossiping about the visitors, Terrin thought.

She had noticed many people staring. Arnold seemed to be getting the most attention. Swamp people were short and lithe, and he was anything but. Also, the way he kept glancing warily towards the platform's edge no doubt seemed humorous to them.

Nora and Chris had come to explore the shops. Nora was haggling with the herbalist, while Chris admired the selection of fruit.

But Terrin's interest lay with Ceianna, who had planted herself near the edge of the platform, standing guard over her charges with arms crossed. Terrin had been considering trying a tactical approach, but she decided that tactical was not her specialty. Not when it came to people. She strode to Ceianna, brushing her hair back over her shoulders as she went.

Ceianna glanced up, her lips tightening and her eyebrows drawing together.

Terrin crossed her own arms and took a long breath before starting.

"You are the second sentry of Shylak."

"Yes."

"Where's the first sentry?"

"What is that to you?" Ceianna said. Her words were clipped and sharp.

"I was wondering who else is in the swamp."

Terrin let her lips quirk into a taut smile.

"Well, let's see," said Ceianna slowly. "Who else? Oh, yeah, me and everyone else who lives in Shylak. If you must know, though, the first sentry is out on patrol."

"Which is exactly why neither you, nor the elder, followed the rules and called him in to keep watch over us. I see."

"Rules?" Ceianna said, a frown creasing her face.

"The charge of any visitors to the swamp shall fall upon the first sentry, unless he is otherwise detained," quoted Terrin. "Do you want me to continue? It's rather long, as laws generally are."

Ceianna's frown deepened for a moment, and then she tilted her head back a bit and smiled. "If that was swamp law, not only would you have no business knowing it, but you would also have no business knowing who else was in the swamp. Any other, less invasive, questions?"

"Well, I was wondering whe—"

"Terrin?" cried a familiar voice.

Terrin spun just in time to be pulled into a crushing hug by Zuen. He released her and took a step back, looking her over.

"You get older every time I see you," he said.

Terrin pursed her lips, and planted her fists against her hips. "That is how it works, Zuen. Time passes and people age. And I thought you were the wise one."

Zuen laughed, and Terrin couldn't stop the smile that split her face.

"You two know each other?" said Ceianna. Her frown had returned.

"Yes," said Zuen. "I often visit her village. Side effect of being a merchant."

"I see. That does explain some things."

Terrin smirked. "Like how I know swamp laws? Oh, wait, I don't because they don't exist."

Zuen put an arm tightly around Terrin's shoulders—with some difficulty, since he was shorter than her.

"I see you two are hitting it off about as well as should be expected." He started to pull Terrin away. "I think I shall steal Terrin, if you don't mind. My wife has always wanted to meet her."

"Fine," said Ceianna.

She turned sharply and walked off towards the others.

∽

"It's unfortunate that you were paired with Ceianna," Zuen said. "I would recommend avoiding conversation with her in the future."

"Why?" asked Terrin.

They were sitting in the small kitchen of Zuen's house. His wife, Melana, was heating water for tea.

"Well, you know how our two peoples used to be constantly warring, right?"

"Until the plainsmen came from across the sea and earned our loyalty, and we made one of them the first ruler of North

Raec, and promised to make peace between our two races," Terrin recited with a smile.

"Well, that was ages ago," he said, "and most of both peoples have forgotten, or don't care. However there are a couple families who—well, they still remember. One family in particular has more or less made it their job to continue loathing the forest people."

"Doesn't that destroy the purpose of the peace?" asked Terrin.

Melana laughed, and both Terrin and Zuen looked at her.

"I'm sorry," she said. "It's just that I've tried telling them that. But Zalisha seems to think that giving up past enmity would destroy part of what we are."

"Who?" asked Terrin.

This time Zuen answered. "Ceianna's grandmother. She has a crazy hatred of your people that she's trying to pass on to her granddaughter. Unfortunately, Ceianna's mother and father are both dead."

"It's a pity," said Melana, setting out their teacups and beginning to pour. The scent of herbs flooded Terrin's nose. "Ceianna's a good girl, really, and her mother was a lovely woman who would have taught her not to fall for that silly prejudice. But she's grown up too serious. She forgets what it is to be of the swamp, what should define us. And with her grandmother, well…"

Melana's voice trailed off, and they sipped their tea in silence.

Something nagged at the corner of Terrin's mind, a detail or connection she ought to notice. But she couldn't grasp it, so instead she asked the question that had been on the tip of her tongue since before Zuen had dragged her here.

"Zuen, you've studied the lore of the swamp, right? I was wondering, what is the biggest tree in the area? Circumference-wise, I mean. And that might be of some significance to your people."

Zuen leaned back, his eyes looking her over. Then he glanced at Melana. She took a sip of her tea, then gave a short nod.

He began to speak, and from the tone of his voice, Terrin anticipated a long story.

"Well I have never seen it. No one has—or at least no one will admit they have. But there are legends of one tree…"

∾ 30 ∾

Christopher

The inside of the council tree was hollowed out evenly, its walls and floor polished smooth. Beneath Chris's feet, the tree rings showed exactly how ancient the tree was. A staircase wound around the wall.

It had been more than two months since he had last climbed stairs, and, by the time he reached the meeting room, he was winded. A stitch poked his side.

Instead of chairs, there were cushions arranged on the floor. It had always been a custom of the swamp people to leave themselves fully visible at official meetings, as a sign of trust. The elder they'd met before and two slightly younger men had already taken their seats.

Chris lowered himself and mirrored their cross-legged posture. The others sat as well—except for Ceianna, who stood by the stairs.

The elder gestured to the cups of tea in front of their seats.

"Please, drink. The climb can be quite tiring."

Chris obediently took a long sip. It was soothing, and the stitch faded within seconds of the liquid hitting his stomach.

"So, what has brought you to the swamp?"

"My friends and I are on a quest," he began.

In the corner of his eye, he could see Terrin spinning her cup in her hand. She had been fidgety since she returned the evening before but had brushed off his attempts to question her. He continued slowly, not taking his eyes off the elder's face. This part sounded strange no matter how many times he said it.

"We believe that we have found the riddles that King Miles followed, that led him to the Stone. We decided to follow these riddles ourselves, and they have brought us here."

A light sparked in the elder's eyes, and he leaned forward a bit. "A riddle? May we hear it?"

Chris let his eyes slide shut as he began to recite.

> "Ho ho he he ha ha ho ho.
> Twiddle your thumbs and dance.
> Winter winds freeze away.
> And sun doth rain its golden heat.
> And I will laugh all day with
> Ho ho he he ha ha ho ho,
> And I will laugh all day!"

Chris opened his eyes. He was surprised to see the elder's own eyes had fallen shut. The three swamp men began to chant.

> "Ho ho he he ha ha ho ho.
> There be work to do, but nay.
> Spring doth already fade,
> And so many things need doing,
> But I shall laugh all day, with
> Ho ho he he ha ha ho ho,

And I will laugh all day!

"Ho ho he he ha ha ho ho.
Fish do beg to be caught,
Summer be a going,
And they be hop, hop, hoppin'.
Though I do laugh all day, with
Ho ho he he ha ha ho ho,
And I will laugh all day!

"Ho ho he he ha ha ho ho.
Now time be runnin' out,
Fall is going by,
And winter may freeze hope.
Yet still I laugh all day, with
Ho ho he he ha ha ho ho.
Aye, I will laugh all day!"

As the song ended, the elder's head began to nod. He opened his eyes, and leaned back, his head bumping against the smooth interior of the tree.

"Yes, indeed, your logic seems sound. And I believe we can help you. Though—"

The man straightened and folded his hands across his lap. His eyes seemed to bore into Chris.

In the thick silence that fell, Chris's mind raced through everything he had learned of the swamp people, wondering if there was some custom he was forgetting.

The seconds ticked by until the elder spoke again.

"You and, excepting Thomas, your friends are very young," he said, and his eyes went from one of them to the next. "Yet you are on a quest first taken by King Miles many generations ago. Tell me, for I can't help but be curious, why did you start on this quest?

How did you find this riddle? So many have searched for it, yet failed, but you…"

"It was sheer luck. No, not luck, some sort of magic. No—" Chris paused. In reality he had been kidnapped by harpies, but that was a story all its own.

A smile tugged the men's features at his hesitation.

Gathering his wits, he began again.

"We have found two riddles. We were led to the first one by magic—and some help. And when we found it, only I could read it. To my friends, it was in a strange tongue. We interpreted it, and then followed the clues to the second riddle. Again, only I could read it, and it was as you heard.

"In both cases, the riddles were surrounded by powerful magic. And I believe this, or some other magic, has been guiding us along the way—"

He stopped again.

He had not actually had a dream since just after the second riddle, and that had been of little use.

Was the magic still guiding them?

"And?" the elder said. He had once again leaned forward.

Chris mentally shook himself.

"And those facts have led me to believe that I—with the aid of my friends—" he added forcefully, and in the corner of his eyes he saw Nora smile, "—am meant to be following the riddles."

The elder's gaze continued to bore into him for what felt like hours.

Finally, the man spoke.

"I feel like there is a very interesting story to be told here, and I would one day like to hear it in full. Of course, no doubt, if these truly are King Miles's ancient riddles, it will be written down in a book. If so, I hope someone of the swamp will write it. You plainsmen make history sound so dull and dry."

The other men nodded.

"But for now," the elder continued, "I have heard enough. I will accept your friendship and give you aid.

"In swamp lore there is an… archaic entity. It is said that this creature acted as guardian of the swamp people in their early days. The entity is called Ho ho he he ha ha ho ho. The same Ho ho he he ha ha ho ho in the song.

"Deep in the swamp, there is a place where no one goes, where the being is said to have lived. If you wish, Ceianna will take you there. I cannot, of course, promise you success in your quest. But if you fail, it shall not be my fault. You may go."

Chris and the others stood, and Ceianna started down the stairs. But as he stepped away, he paused, his conscience stabbing his heart.

He turned back to the elder.

"I have offered you friendship," he said, "but it cannot be true friendship if I do not tell you the consequences that come with it."

The elder's eyebrows arched.

Chris straightened his back and took a deep breath before finishing.

"My full name was Honorable Christopher Fredrico, son of Earl Fredrico. However, more than two months ago, I was suspected for the theft of the Shard that rested in my city. I was banished by Prince Tyler—given only one month to leave the country.

"I assure you that I did not commit this crime, and it is part of why this quest is important to me. But if knowing this means you must take back your offer of aid, then… I would ask that you at least allow me to continue my search on my own."

ભ 31 ભ

Terrin

The raft cruised through the water with Ceianna's deter-mined strokes. The girl's face had been stony since the elder announced that she would guide them to the tree.

The tree was amazingly well hidden, despite its size. The other trees clustered around, making it impossible to see its true width until you were within a few yards. Terrin knew at once it was the tree from her dream. Besides the enormity of the trunk and the large, carved door, she could sense the sameness of the tree—or maybe that was just the magic flowing from it.

The group trooped off the boat solemnly, staring up at the large tree. Even Terrin, though she had seen it before, couldn't help but be awed by it.

"Well," said Arnold, "either this is it, or I'm a great big baboon… oh, wait—Well, guess this isn't it."

Everyone shifted their stares to him, and Terrin rolled her eyes.

"Congrats," she said, "you get the Worst Joke Ever award."

Chris shook his head, and stepped towards the door.

"Let's go in. Like Arnold said, this is it. It feels just like before."

He placed one hand on the wood and pushed for a second, with no results. He threw his weight against it. The door did not budge.

"I should have mentioned," said Ceianna. "That door, it has never been opened."

"It's a door. Of course it's been opened," snapped Terrin.

Chris frowned at her slightly as he stepped away from the tree.

Thomas quickly said, "That is a good point. Why make a door, if not to open it? And for another thing, if this is the location for the next riddle, then King Miles must have got in somehow."

"The question is," said Chris, "how do we open it now?"

Terrin started to examine the door when a thought struck her. Slowly she stepped away from the tree and looked across the waters to the other isle in the dream, where the wraith and the old woman had been.

Where the wraith and the old woman were now.

Terrin's heart caught in her throat, thinking for a moment it was the same woman from the dream who now glowered at them. Then she realized that the truth was even more frightening—this woman was the same as had watched her back in Xell.

"Chris, can you read the inscription?" said Nora, distracting Terrin. "It looks a bit like swamp script, but it's not familiar."

Terrin glanced up at the swirls above the door and realized that they were indeed words.

"No, can't read it," said Chris, frowning.

"I can," said Terrin, as she realized that they were not only words, but words she recognized.

Ceianna arched her eyebrows.

"It's ancient swamp script," Terrin continued. "For Laughter will this door open, Laughter with ho ho he he ha ha ho ho always in hand."

"Maybe it means you need the entity to open it," said Ceianna. "And since Ho ho he he ha ha ho ho's not here, we should really all just go home." Her brow was furrowed.

"Or maybe someone should tell a joke," said Arnold. "If I was an ancient entity of protection, what would be my favorite joke?"

While everyone's attention was averted from her, Terrin glanced back to the bushes. The woman and the wraith were gone.

They're probably just my imagination, Terrin told herself. No one else had seen them.

Unless Ceianna had, and that was why she was nervous. Terrin glanced back at the swamp girl. Once again she felt something nagging at the back of her mind, a connection that she ought to make.

"Ceianna, you're the expert here," said Chris. "Do you have any ideas?"

"Well," she said, rubbing her hands together as if they were cold, "I would not say I'm an expert. However, in the inscription, Laughter is used as a name, not as an action. Also..." She paused here, chewing her lip.

"Also?" said Chris softly.

"I don't think ho ho he he ha ha ho ho does refer to the entity," she said quickly, and flushed slightly.

Terrin glanced back at the inscription. "She's right."

"What does that mean?" said Nora.

There was a long silence, and Terrin gave up on the nagging feeling, and turned her attention to the problem at hand. In the dream, no one else had showed up, certainly not any ancient entities. No, one of the companions had opened the door.

Reluctantly she recalled the dream's details, searching for clues. She was sure the stocky young man had opened it, but how? Some particular way of touching the carvings? And why was Laughter used as a na— "Oh! I see," said Terrin.

The others all stared at her.

"Names and titles are basically the same thing in the ancient swamp tongue. And titles are just descriptions of what you are or do. So it would mean someone who is known for causing laughter. And I think," she couldn't help smiling as she finished, "that we all know who that is."

"Huh," said Arnold, cracking a grin. "Nope, still don't get it."

Terrin glared at him, but he was already moving towards the door. He didn't even touch the wood before the door swung open, just like in the dream. Magic seemed to exhale from the room beyond, sending tingles up and down her spine.

They filed through the door into a round room. It was not as big as the size of the tree might have led her to expect, most of the space being taken up with a broad spiral stair case similar to that in the council tree. The walls and floor were all smooth, but instead of the gray of the council tree, they were a sandy brown color, as if this tree were somehow still alive.

Terrin thought she felt the floor pulse under her feet, though she couldn't be sure.

When they reached the middle of the room, the door swung shut, silent until the clunk as it fell into place. They looked back, and Terrin was unsettled to see that the inside of the door was exactly like the rest of the wall. It was impossible to tell where it had been.

Though there was no obvious source of light, the room was still bright. Magic seemed to emanate from the wood itself, sending shivers up and down Terrin's spine in a way that she thought only spirits could.

"Of course," said Arnold, looking up the stairs. "It would be too easy to put the riddle on the first floor."

PART THREE

Terrin, 8 years earlier

The oak was beautiful, the tallest tree Terrin had ever seen, and her brother's fingers barely brushed the lowest branch.

"Trunnen, if you fall, I will not be held accountable," Terrin said, her hands planted on her hips.

"Good thing I won't fall," Trunnen said, gazing from his perch on a large rock.

"You're right, you won't. Because you're not going to climb it. Because you're a good child who does what his parents say. Oh wait, that's me."

She waved a handful of the water-wort they'd been sent to fetch. "We should go back to the village. Mother will wonder why we are taking so long. Or did you forget we're on an errand?"

They had had to go several miles out to find the herb, and the sun was already well on its downward track.

"This won't take long. I won't go all the way up," Trunnen said.

"And Mother wonders why we can't get along. You're no fun."

Terrin crossed her arms. "Father will find out, somehow. He always does."

"Well, it won't be from my mouth. So unless it's from yours, how could he?"

He crouched, and sprang straight up, his hands reaching for the branch.

His fingers closed around the limb's bark, and a victorious grin split his face—for a second. The expression contorted as his feet scrambled for purchase against the tree trunk. Then his fingers slipped from the limb and he fell to the ground, tumbling over.

Terrin laughed. "I told you you'd fall."

Trunnen slowly picked himself up, scowling slightly.

"I can climb it. That rock just wasn't big enough."

"Well, we definitely do not have time to find another one, so let's go."

She turned away.

"Wait, I want to try one more thing first. I saw someone in another village do it. I've wanted to try it for a while now."

"Then can we go?" Terrin ask, glancing back at him.

"Yes," he said.

He bent down and rolled the boulder slightly to the side.

"Fine."

She turned back to watch. He moved as far back from the oak as he could, dancing on his toes slightly. A glint shone in his eye.

"What are you doing?" Terrin asked.

Instead of answering, he just grinned and started to run. His feet churned over the ground as he narrowed in on the tree.

Then, a few feet away, he leaned back and without slowing down he set one foot against the tree trunk. Using his momentum he pressed his foot into the trunk and pulled his other foot up after it. He started to take a third step. His hand reached to wrap around the branch.

Her breath caught in her throat. How could he run up the tree?

Then the smooth leather sole of his shoe slipped.

"That was never going to—"

He hit the ground with a sharp thud.

"Trunnen!" she cried, dropping the water-wort.

Though he'd moved the rock to clear his path, he had not moved it far. When he fell, he clipped his head against its edge.

She dashed to his side, dropping to her knees as she reached him. She touched his shoulder. His eyes were shut, and he made no response.

"Trunnen, get up. I told you it was a bad idea, you idiot."

Then she noticed a red puddle growing around his head, and she felt her own blood drain from her face. Her throat tightened.

"I have to stop the bleeding," she said weakly.

She lifted his head and pressed her hand against the wound. She cringed at the warm, sticky feeling as the blood oozed through her fingers. She couldn't stop the flow. For a minute, she struggled against throwing up.

"I'm not afraid of blood," she said, staring at the puddle.

How many times had she killed and cleaned animals? How was their blood any different from this?

But it was different, and she couldn't stand it anymore. She pulled away, franticly wiping her hand against her leggings. She turned her eyes away from the blood, fighting to hold back both her stomach and her tears.

"Trunnen, please wake up. I don't know what to do."

How could she stop the blood when she couldn't stand to look at it? But if she didn't do something, he would probably bleed out before she could get help.

The only thing she could think of was to scream, and hope someone was near enough to hear.

She lifted her head. Her jaw dropped open.

She blinked.

A slight, gray man sat on a pony, with a second pony tied behind, covered in baggage. His gaze swept between her and Trunnen. The man was covered in mud. A swamp man.

"Who are you?" Terrin asked, standing and crossing her arms.

He swung off the horse, and bowed slightly.

"My name is Zuen. I am a merchant. I offer my assistance."

Terrin's throat tightened as she fought for a second with her instinct to distrust strangers. But what choice did she have? She glanced once at Trunnen, and quickly looked away.

"Please," she said softly.

"Hold my horse," Zuen said.

She took the reins, and he went to his saddle bag. Though she generally disliked the large creatures, Terrin found herself burying her face in the warm neck of the horse she held.

"Get on the pony," said Zuen, after a minute.

Terrin looked up. Zuen held Trunnen, whose head was now bandaged.

"Why?"

"Because he needs to be kept upright, to minimize the blood loss. I don't want him in the saddle alone, and I will not ride while you walk."

With a short nod, Terrin clambered into the saddle. Zuen lifted Trunnen up in front of her and took the reins.

"You know the forest well, do you not?" Zuen asked.

"Y-yes."

"We need to get your friend to a healer quickly. Will you

guide me?"

"Yes." Terrin thought for a second, then pointed. "That way. And he's not my friend, he's my brother."

"I see. Thank you."

He clucked the horses into a brisk walk, then added, "Luck is on your brother's side, since he chose the very week I started my merchant life to be injured. And besides that, you both strike me as strong-willed young people. He will be fine."

Terrin nodded.

ℭᴐ 33 ℭᴐ

Trillory

"For the last time, no," Trill said. She sent a glaring glance over her shoulder at him, then continued to read her book.

With little else to do around the manor, she spent most of her afternoons in the mage room, watching Eric practice. But today, he had been continually pausing to pester her about learning magic.

Across the room, Eric muttered over a stone cupped in his hands.

"From stone to wood. From rock to wood. From stone to wood. From rock to wood."

Finally Trill's curiosity got the best of her.

"Won't the spell wear off?"

"No, once the properties of an object are changed, they stay changed. Once the magic from the casting fades, someone would have to cast another spell to change it back."

"I see. What about before the magic fades?"

"They could reverse the spell. It would take more control than casting a new spell, but in other ways it would be easier."

There was a slight change in his tone that made Trill glance at him again. He was watching her with an amused smile.

"What?" she said.

"Nothing. I just thought you didn't want to learn magic, that's all."

Trill stared at him. He continued to smile back.

She let out a long sigh.

"I don't. I was just curious."

"Mhm," he said, turning back to his rock and taking up the chant again.

When his magic continued to fail for several minutes, he finally joined her at the small table, pouring himself a glass of water from the ever-present pitcher. Trill stared at the book without really seeing the words. She could feel him watching her, but she refused to meet his gaze.

Finally Eric spoke. "Why not? You obviously don't have anything against the use of magic, or you wouldn't be here. So why don't you want to learn?"

She leaned back and looked at him, turning her answer over in her mind.

"I guess," she finally said, "I don't want to learn something that I'll never use."

"You don't know that."

"When would I use it?" she challenged, leaning forward a bit.

"You could have used it with the bear. Or for fun."

"For fun? I don't want to learn magic just to use 'for fun.'"

"What would make it different from any other hobby? Like your gardening. You'd just be nurturing a talent you already have."

"Because..."

She paused. He had a point. A small one.

"Because?"

"Because I don't want to use something like magic for a hobby. Especially not when a war is coming on. If there's a war, the king could use a good magician like your father. Or you. But does even the king know? Are you going to tell him?"

Eric was silent, his eyes lowered to the table, where his fingers traced its grain.

Trill watched him, letting the silence thicken till it was a heavy blanket that pushed down on her, making it hard to breathe. Finally he glanced up.

"I don't know what we'll say. That is up to my father."

"Well, I don't want to have a talent like that, only to hide it from those I could help."

"Why should you hide it? Surely not just because my father chooses to do so? He has no control over you."

"My father hates magic. He barely tolerates its use for common wards. Even if I did learn magic—even if I tried to offer my services to the king—my father wouldn't let me. He'd be horrified with me. So I'd rather not learn."

"So instead of having a talent and not using it, you're just going to deny ever having it?"

"No!"

Trill dropped her book, and despite the fact that it was mere inches from the table, its clunk sounded like thunder to her. She met his eyes and held them for a minute.

Then she sighed. "That's not it."

"I think it is."

The blanket of silence returned.

After several minutes, Eric tried again.

"All I want to say is that maybe you should give it a chance. Learn to use your talent, and then at that point you can decide what to do with it. Would that really be so bad? Besides, if you wanted to use your magic for the king, would you really let your father stop you?"

Trill shifted her gaze to stare over his shoulder, tears of frustration and confusion welling in her eyes. Her eyelids slid shut as she breathed deeply, forcing herself to clear her muddled mind and think.

Then she met his eyes.

"You said earlier that reversing a spell took more control, but was easier. What does that mean?"

A grin cut Eric's face from ear to ear, and he quickly launched into an explanation. "There are two main aspects to a magician's ability: their skill at controlling and focusing the magic, but also how much power they have available. To reverse the spell, you'd just be dispersing the magic, so you wouldn't be expending much power.

"Some people are natural at control, others have lots of power. You seem to have a good bit of both. Which is good, because if you have control but not power, you might learn quickly, but you can't exactly learn more power, just how to conserve what you have. But if you have power, but no control, then you're like me, and even simple spells take effort. In that case…"

Trill couldn't help but smile at his eagerness.

He may struggle with spells, she thought, *but he's not a half bad teacher.*

∽ 34 ∽

Brayden

"The ambassador—" King Orin paused shortly, then moved on, "—ors from North Raec may now speak."

Brayden sat next to Gillian Fredrico, the original ambassador. Of course, Gillian was still the official ambassador. But it would seem odd if the prince, after coming all this way, didn't meet with the king.

Gillian stood and bowed.

"M'lords," he began. "There has been a great tragedy. A party of North Raecan merchants was attacked and slaughtered. In their investigations of the scene, our officials discovered evidence that there may have been South Raecan involvement."

Gillian managed to cover his anger, to a degree, but Brayden knew that everyone present could hear the tightness in his voice. There was a moment of silence as the king and all present mulled over this. Gillian's eyes remained locked on the king.

Brayden would have found the situation unbearably intense, had his palms not decided to start itching. Nervous energy. After a minute of resisting the urge to rub his hands under the ornately carved table, he began to wonder if he should say something.

Orin finally made a response. "Are you suggesting something, Ambassador?"

The king's tone was lower than it had been all day, and that sent more tingles through Brayden's hands.

"Nothing at all, King Orin," said Gillian smoothly. "We merely wish to inquire whether you might know anything of the situation."

This time, the tingles went through Brayden's spine.

One of the younger lords stood. The man had been alert since the king announced that it was the North Raecans' turn to speak. Now he slapped the table with both hands.

"How dare you imply that His Majesty's court had anything to do with this attack?"

"I only stated that a South Raecan insignia had been found at the scene. We are not implying anything."

"You're right. You practically shouted the accusation in our faces. As if we would waste our time with your people. I bet you're just dying to draw us into a fight, hoping to grow rich on plunder."

"You say we're eager to start a war?" Gillian leaned toward the young lord, his knuckles white where his fists pressed against the table. "Who was it that attacked first?"

Brayden's hands had stopped itching. His eyes were turned towards Orin, who was watching the two younger men face off. A frown etched itself deeper and deeper into the king's face. The other lords were either leaning back to stay out of the way, or leaning in, ready to join the argument.

Brayden reacted almost without thinking. He stood and grabbed Gillian's shoulder. The ambassador was almost ten years older, but Brayden was nearly as tall, and the movement caught

Gillian by surprise. He stepped back.

The South Raecan lord froze, staring.

The king spoke, one eyebrow slightly raised. "Prince Brayden?"

Brayden swallowed, fighting to keep his voice calm.

"We are not accusing anyone, sir," he said. "Nor do we want a war. It never entered our minds that the nobles of South Raec had known of the attack."

Ignoring murmurs around the table, he fixed his attention on the king. "However, since the rogues appear to have come from your land, King Orin, we were hoping to gain your assistance in tracking them down before they cause further trouble."

He spread his hands in a gesture of peace. "We are not trying to incite a war. We're trying to prevent one."

Brayden took a deep breath and sat down, making sure that Gillian came with him. The ambassador looked just as stunned as everyone else at the table—except for Orin, whose face had become unreadable.

Brayden waited, surprised that his voice hadn't been squeaky.

The king coughed.

"Baron Torc," he said, "please be seated."

The young noble jerked backwards out of his stupor and sat down hard. Brayden could see a light blush beginning to brighten the man's cheeks.

Orin stood, turning towards Brayden and giving a slight bow.

"Prince Brayden, I'm sure that what you say is true. I shall, of course, tell my men to discretely search for any rumors of such a renegade force. I hope I may soon have news for you to take back to your father.

"While you are here, I would like very much to discuss some terms of a treaty I've been considering, which I hope your father will agree with. A treaty that will bring both Raecs great prosperity and peace."

Brayden stood and bowed deeper.

"I would be greatly honored to talk of such a treaty—" he paused, feeling Gillian's gaze. "But, ah, I feel it would be best if I consult with advisers before entering any negotiation. I had not intended to stay very long, and I may not be able to change my plans."

"Of course."

Brayden sat, and the king moved on to the next order of business. After a minute his hands started itching again, and the restless tingle spread to his neck and back. He could feel Gillian's glare. Not that he could blame the ambassador. He was sure that his father's letter had said Brayden was not to interfere.

Perhaps his father hadn't known about a particular young, volatile baron, or about the tension within the South Raecan court.

ᕥ 35 ᕥ

Nora

Arnold shrugged and started up the stairs. The others stood in a sort of shock for a moment, and then Chris followed him. Thomas went next, and then Terrin. The forest girl's pace was forced, and her face looked pale.

Nora advanced cautiously. Though she did not share her friend's fear of magic, this place set her skin crawling. There had been powerful magic surrounding the riddles before, but it hadn't seemed active, just there. But this magic shifted around them, and Nora thought she could feel it brush against her skin. And then there was the light—at the last cave, there had also been unnatural light, but at least it had seemed to have a source.

Something moved in the corner of her eye, and she glanced around.

It was only Ceianna.

The swamp girl seemed as reluctant as Terrin to climb the stairs. She kept glancing back to where the door had been, and the strands of her long hair swirled in disarray.

The others slowed as the stairs passed a side room, but a quick glance convinced them that the riddle was not there. They pressed on.

Nora hung slightly back.

"Ceianna?" she said, softly.

"Yes?" the girl replied sharply.

Nora flinched. The other swamp people had been easy to talk to, welcoming. But Ceianna's tone seemed ever sharp and defensive.

"I was just wondering, if you're scared of this place, why did you come with us?"

Ceianna tossed her head, swinging the hair back away from her face. "I'm not afraid of the tree. Was it not the home of the swamp people's protector?"

Nora walked a couple more steps, before her curiosity again outweighed her shyness. "Then why are you nervous?"

Ceianna scowled at her. "You people sure ask a lot of questions. But if you must know, I'm not afraid of the tree, but of the consequences of letting your group enter it. But I'm here because while you're in the swamp you are my charges, and I must do my best to protect you. And to keep you out of trouble."

"Oh," said Nora. "But aren't your people loyal to the crown? And Chris…"

"Would you prefer that we locked your friend in chains and handed him over?"

"No, of course not!" Nora said.

She blushed and glanced forward, but the others had climbed out of sight. She looked back at Ceianna.

"Chris is our people's friend now," the swamp girl said. "And, like you, the elder believes his innocence. Unless the king himself gives us a direct order, we will keep our word to help him find the riddle. And I must do my part."

A smile spread across the girl's face. "If the elder had not believed Chris's innocence... Well, it would have been a different story."

"Oh."

"Come, we are falling behind," said Ceianna.

Nora's legs were starting to get tired, but she forced herself to pick up the pace. Ceianna seemed barely touched by the climb. They passed another empty room.

A few steps later there was a cry from above. All weariness vanished from Nora as she stormed up the stairs. Pulling out her dagger, she took the steps two at a time, with Ceianna right behind her.

A wall rose from the next platform's floor to its roof, blocking their view until they rounded the corner. The stairs ended in an alcove of sorts, which opened into a room the full width of the tree, with smooth, polished walls all around. On the far wall, Nora saw Arnold standing at the base of another set of stairs that spiraled up into darkness. A jagged fence of branches seemed to be growing from the floor, blocking him off from the rest of the friends. He was sawing at it with his knife.

He looked up at Nora and shouted, "Move!"

At the same moment, Nora saw the edges of the alcove warping. She grabbed Ceianna's arm and rushed into the room as a branch sprang across the doorway.

To her left, Thomas had been wrapped in root-like tentacles, which were pulling him towards the wall. Chris had his sword out and was hacking at them, trying to free him. On her right, more of the tentacles were sprouting out of the floor and waving toward her, but she danced nimbly, swinging her long dagger at any that came too close.

Nora switched her dagger to the other hand and drew her sword. Ceianna was already rushing towards Thomas and Chris, so she turned to help Terrin, who was surrounded by waving tentacles that seemed to be herding her towards the side wall. When their blades struck at a root, it would pull back but immediately lunge forward again. The metal barely scratched the living wood. The one time Nora's blade did cut in an inch, she nearly didn't get it back before the root pulled away.

A tentacle lunged for her, and she beat it away, and then stepped back for a second to get her bearings.

"Terrin, the wall!" she cried.

The wall itself was writhing as more tentacles sprouted and reached for the girl. Terrin glanced round and jumped away, slashing at the new foes. Another tentacle sprang up from the front to grab her, and Nora leaped forward, slashing at it.

The root pulled back and turned towards her. When it lunged for her, she jumped sideways to avoid it. But another one swept from behind, knocking her to the floor, and a third snatched the sword from her loosened grip and tossed it away.

Nora caught herself with her hands, and then bunched her muscles to surge back to her feet.

But she couldn't move.

The floor had grown around her hands and lower legs, holding her in place.

ↂ 36 ↂ

Arnold

Arnold's sword did nothing against the wood that blocked his way. Its crisscrossing pattern made it hard to strike, and the limbs had hardened into place. He had tried hacking and stabbing, but nothing helped. He'd even sawed at the thing with his knife. That had gotten nearly half way through one of the limbs, but then the wood had grown up and engulfed the blade.

So he watched helplessly as his friends battled the tree.

Only Ceianna seemed to be having any success. She had charged into freeing Thomas, and her knife flashed white as she struck the tentacles left and right. Her hair swung around but never seemed to get in the way.

But what was strange was that when she struck a tentacle, it actually withdrew. Several roots curled near the floor and wall, withered from her blows, though they seemed to be slowly recovering.

Chris was doing his best to watch her back, but his blade was as useless as Arnold's.

Terrin was having a bit more success. She nimbly avoided the tentacles that reached for her, even causing a few of them to get confused and tangle with each other. And her knife was striking deeper than the swords while still sliding free easily. But the tentacles didn't wither, just flinched away for a moment.

Nora was still struggling against the floor. Only her hands and lower legs were covered, but it was enough that she could not pull free.

"Chris, Thomas," said Ceianna, "Try now."

She spun and thrust her knife into one of the tentacles holding Thomas. He fell forward, and Chris caught him and pulled. It was enough. They surged free of the wood, and Ceianna pulled her knife back as the roots retreated.

The three paused to catch their breath, and for a second Arnold thought the tree was doing the same.

Then the floor seemed to ripple.

"Keep moving," he shouted.

Chris glanced down. The floor was starting to melt around his feet. He jerked free, and the others danced away.

The tree shook a bit, and then more tentacles lunged for them.

"Ceianna, free Nora," said Chris, beating one off. "Then try and get through to Arnold.

Ceianna nodded and practically leaped to Nora's side. She knelt and began to stab at the floor, carefully avoiding Nora's hand. The wood grew up around her calves, but she ignored it. The floor did not retreat from the knife as the tentacles had, but the knife sliced it well enough, and it did not grow back.

Arnold scanned the room.

"Chris, Thomas, watch it!" he called as a tentacle lunged from behind them.

Chris turned and beat it off. At the same time Thomas leaped sideways, avoiding another tentacle but narrowly missing Chris.

And moving himself closer to Terrin.

"Chris," Arnold called. "They're trying to group you together."

Chris glanced around and nodded. "Spread out! We'll only get in each other's way." Then he lunged through a tight group of tentacles and away from Thomas. One caught around his chest, but he struck it with his sword and pulled free.

Ceianna had managed to release Nora's hands and was working at her legs.

They were running out of time. The roots were multiplying. Every few moments, more would surge from the walls, floor, or even the ceiling. And the ones Ceianna had decommissioned were moving again.

Then Nora was free. She jumped to her feet, the layer of wood that had surrounded her legs cracking into splinters that seemed to melt back into the floor.

Ceianna spun the knife and handed it to Nora hilt first.

"Go to Arnold," she said. "Get that door open."

Nora frowned. "But you're—"

"It won't matter, if that door isn't open soon. Remember what I said before."

Nora still frowned, but she turned and dashed across the room to the stairway and began to stab at it. The limbs of wood reluctantly shriveled away from it, but it would obviously take time.

Arnold moved to the side so he could see around her. Still, he couldn't see much. Terrin was completely out of sight, Chris and Thomas in and out of it. He could tell they were both slowing down. Thomas was old, and neither was trained for this type of combat—or much of any combat.

Ceianna, at the other edge of his vision, was trying to pull herself free, but she had no weapon to cut away the wood. Then a simple-handled knife thudded into the floor, an inch from her leg, and splintered the wood. Ceianna glanced up to where Arnold knew Terrin must be. Then she snatched up the knife and began cutting her way free.

"Through!" Nora shouted as she clambered into the stairway.

She had only cut away a couple of the middle limbs, but it was enough. She stood panting for a second, then shifted her feet experimentally.

"Give me the knife and keep going," said Arnold.

"What?" said Nora, though she handed over the knife obediently.

"The stairway isn't wide enough for us all to go up at once, and there's only one knife. Just keep going."

Nora hesitated for a moment, then nodded and ran up the stairs.

Already the doorway was resealing itself. Arnold braced his left forearm against the wall, then thrust at the regrowing limbs angrily.

"You are going to let us go if it's the last thing you do," he said, striking it with each word.

Ceianna leaped to her feet, the wood shattering as it had done with Nora. She ran across the room but stopped outside of the door, joining Arnold in his efforts to keep back the blockade. Once again the floor began to reseal around her feet.

"Come through before you get stuck again," said Arnold.

"No. The two of us on the other side would block the stairway."

"Then come through and keep going up," he insisted.

"No."

Thomas reached the door and jumped through the opening. Chris was right behind him, but he glanced back to where Terrin was still avoiding the tentacles.

"Terrin—" he said and moved towards her, but Thomas reached back, snatched his shirt, and pulled him to the door.

"Can't be helped right now," said the older man. Chris reluctantly clambered through, and Arnold moved aside to let them both run up the stairs.

"Terrin, come on!" he called.

Terrin glanced up at him. She had been nimbly avoiding the tentacles, but they would soon cut off her escape route. She turned and loped across the room, dodging under and around and even just pushing past the tentacles that reached for her. Without even pausing, she jumped feet first through the hole, catching the upper limb with her arm so that when her feet touched the floor she did not fall.

"What about Ceianna?" she asked.

"Just run," hissed the girl, tossing her head back. "I am the second sentry of Shylak. I will be fine."

Terrin gave her a short look, then nodded. She turned to start up the stairs.

Arnold extended the knife towards Ceianna, but she shook her head.

"Keep it. You'll need it," she said, looking over his shoulder. "Go help your friends."

Arnold followed her gaze and saw the stairway walls were rippling. He glanced at Ceianna one last time.

"*Run!*" she shouted, and her voice carried the authority of command that no person with military training could ignore.

He turned and fled up the stairs, taking them three at a time.

Christopher

Chris glanced back over his shoulder and was pleased to see Terrin coming up the stairs. Then his pleasure vanished as Ceianna's cry rang out. He exploded forward, but his breathing was ragged and his legs screamed in rebellion.

Thomas's toe caught the edge of a stair, and he stumbled. Chris grabbed his arm to pull him up. The old man's face was red, and he was breathing heavily, but recovered his balance and kept running.

The wall rippled, and root tentacles began to sprout all around them.

"Faster!" Chris shouted. Even as he spoke, Terrin pressed past him.

A root struck him from behind, knocking his breath out of his lungs and pinning him against the edge of a stair.

Terrin turned back.

He tried to shoo her forward, but he couldn't get enough breath to speak.

Arnold supplied the words: "Keep going, Terrin!"

Chris looked back to see his friend charging up the stairs, a white knife flashing in his hand. The tentacles shriveled back before him. As Arnold approached, the root that pinned him pulled back, and Chris quickly scrambled to his feet.

Arnold kept going, zigging past him and Terrin to the front, where more roots were leaping out to block Thomas's way, then dropping back to fend off a tentacle reaching for Terrin.

"Not far, now," said Arnold.

Chris nodded.

As they climbed on, Arnold waltzed up and down, keeping the way clear with more nimbleness than Chris would ever have expected. Then they rounded the final curve, and he could see a room up ahead. Nora waited at the top of the stairway.

As Chris cleared the doorway he turned back, expecting the tentacles to pursue them, but the roots had stopped just outside the doorway. They waved angrily but did not enter the room.

He collapsed to his knees, fighting to catch his breath.

"The magic… it's different here," Terrin said. She was leaning against the wall, her breath coming in ragged gasps. "More like at the other riddles."

Chris tilted his head, trying to feel a difference. Maybe the magic was thicker here. Or maybe it was his imagination. "I'll take your word for it," he said.

"Where's Ceianna?" said Nora.

"We couldn't get her free in time," Terrin said. "She knew we couldn't free her and survive ourselves. She did her job."

Nora slumped to the ground, her face pale. Terrin sat down beside her and hugged her shoulders.

Arnold sat, his back to the wall, glaring at Terrin.

This room was like the ones before, with smooth walls and a

floor stretching the full width of the tree. But in the center of the room, the floor swelled up, making a hump the size of a boulder. Runes were carved across its face, but Chris refused to look at them. The other riddles had stuck in the forefront of his mind, forcing him to think about them. He wasn't ready for that.

Thomas went to the riddle, and knelt. He pulled out a notepad and began to scribble.

Chris walked over to sit by Arnold. "Terrin's right. If we had died trying to save Ceianna, she would be shamed."

"But I'm a knight," said Arnold. "It's my job to save people, too. I could have at least left her the knife."

Chris dropped his gaze to examine the knife. Ceianna's knife. Its blade was white and triangular, and the hilt simple wood. Then he shook his head.

"No. Without that knife, we would never have made it up the stairs. We'll rescue her on our way back down."

"Chris," said Terrin. "I don't think we're going back down."

Chris spun around to look at the stairs. The walls seemed to be melting inward, oozing between the tentacles. In seconds, the way back was just a solid wall. Arnold jumped up and stabbed at it with the knife, but it bounced right off.

"Great, now we're stuck in here," he said.

"Not necessarily," said Nora.

Arnold, Thomas, and Chris turned to look at her. Nora blushed, but pressed on. "I was just thinking of how well hidden the entry door looked from the inside. And before, at the mountain… It's worth looking for another door."

"I think," said Terrin, "that we'd better look fast. Something is happening."

Nora leaped to her feet and started running her hands over the wall.

"Chris, the riddle," said Arnold.

Chris turned to look at the carved hump. As before, the text looked like plain Raecan to him. He read it aloud:

"Air rushing, rushing by.
Faster, faster than the eye.
Far above the deep, deep blue.
Where water splashes at the rocks.
And higher still the great one flies.
Guarding hope as watchmen pose."

There was a long silence. Chris could feel three pairs of eyes watching him. Everyone but Nora was still.

Then Nora spoke. "I found it!" she called, throwing herself against the wall.

There was a screech of the wood rubbing against the floor. Then a door swung open before her, showing a dark, narrow passage, leading down.

"Looks like fun," said Arnold.

"But it's just in time. We need to clear out now," said Terrin.

Then Chris felt it—a surge in the magic, as if it was all gathering at one spot, collecting into itself.

"Go!" he called, jumping over the hump and to the stairs. Nora stepped aside to let him pass. He grabbed her hand and dragged her after him. He heard the thudding boots of the others following.

Then the magic released. It was rushing out around him, as if something had breathed in deeply, and let it out all at once. The same thing had happened at the lake, and it had caused the whole lake to drain. He didn't really want to know what would happen this time. He wasn't sure he had a choice, though.

Then there was a sucking sound.

"Go faster," Arnold called. "It's closing."

A second later, the light coming through from the riddle room was blocked, leaving them in pitch black. Chris plunged forward as quickly as he could, glad for the evenness of the slope and the close walls to brace himself against—and the lack of tentacles trying to block their way. Then he collided with a wall.

"Wait!" cried Nora, as she nearly ran into him.

Chris braced himself and pushed. There was another screech, and then they poured out of the stairway and paused, blinded by the brightness of the entry room.

"Feel for the door," Chris said, running to the wall and rubbing his hands over it.

"And quickly," said Terrin, looking up.

Chris glanced back to see that the passage behind them was thoroughly sealed. The ceiling and the main stairway were melting. The walls pulsed out and rolled down the stairs like a great wave of molten wood.

"Here!" Arnold shouted, as the door swung open before him.

They ran out onto the grass, and then stopped to look back. The wave had reached the bottom of the stairs, and now the floor was pulsing up to meet it.

Then the door slammed shut.

They stood, staring at the tree and panting.

Arnold was still holding Ceianna's knife, his knuckles white.

∾ 38 ∾

Terrin

"Arnold…" murmured Terrin. She hesitantly touched his shoulder. "You did your best."

"My best? What did I do that was my 'best'?" Arnold said, shrugging off her hand.

"You saved us," said Chris, coming up to his other side.

"I said we'd come back for her. If I hadn't taken her knife…"

Arnold ran his fingers along the side of the knife. It was an odd blade, and Terrin couldn't help shivering whenever she looked at it.

"I already said, if you hadn't taken the knife we'd be dead," Chris said.

"Yes. But I didn't know that when I took it. If she had had the knife—"

"It would have been one more thing to carry," said a familiar voice from behind them.

Terrin spun to face the sound. Ceianna. The swamp girl was standing where they had left the raft. She had thrust the paddle into the mud and now leaned into it casually. For the first time Terrin could see the hint of a smile in her eyes that Zuen, and many of the other swamp people, seemed always to possess.

"Bu-wha- how?" spluttered Arnold.

Ceianna shrugged. "After you were gone, the tree let me go. The upper stairway was already sealing shut, so I came down to wait for you. Here, I grabbed these," she turned and knelt, then stood and held out two knives and a sword.

"My knife," said Arnold, stepping forward and carefully taking and sheathing it.

"And Nora's sword," said Ceianna, turning it so Nora could take it hilt first.

"Thank you," murmured Nora, sheathing it.

"And," Ceianna said, turning towards Terrin, "I believe this is yours."

Their eyes met, and for a second she felt like Ceianna was measuring her.

"Thank you," said Terrin.

"No," said Ceianna. "You lost this knife in order to help me. Thank you."

She turned the knife's hilt towards Terrin and smiled.

Terrin took the knife, sliding it into it sheath with a satisfying hiss, and then returned the smile.

"So, what exactly happened?" said Chris.

"As soon as Arnold left, the staircase started sealing up. By the time he was out of sight around the bend, there was no chance of my getting through. The root tendrils just melted back off of me, and they also spit out Arnold's knife. So I collected the weapons and came down to wait. Guess once there wasn't a chance I'd be getting up, the tree didn't care about me."

"No, the magic never cared about you," said Terrin. "I shouldn't have gone in."

"What?" said Arnold.

Ceianna gave a short nod. "Maybe. But then it also attacked Thomas and Chris."

"Because they were too close to me. The magic couldn't seal them off like it did with Arnold, or like it tried with you and Nora."

"What?" said Arnold.

"Oh," said Chris.

Arnold frowned. "Would someone please explain what Terrin's blaming herself for, so I can tell her off?"

"I think," said Thomas, "they're referring to the old war between the swamp and forest peoples, from before the plains people came to Raec. If this is an ancient swamp deity, it is safe to assume that it, or rather any magic it left behind, would remember those days."

"Oh," said Arnold, his eyebrows knitting together. "Well, it doesn't really matter, does it? I mean, we all made it, and we got the riddle."

"So you found it?" said Ceianna.

"Yes," said Chris.

"Then we should be on our way." She stepped back onto the boat and pulled up the paddle in one smooth movement. "I'll be taking you straight out of the swamp, since you found what you needed."

"We won't be returning to Shylak?"

"No. Some soldiers entered the swamp just before you did, and from what you've said, I'm assuming you would like to stay far away from them. Which way are you headed?"

"North," said Chris. "We need to get our horses before we do anything else."

"Right. If we leave now and travel through the night, you should be out of the swamp before lunch tomorrow."

Christopher

Chris shifted and pulled his blanket tighter around him. Warmth wasn't an issue in the muggy swamp, but it felt strange to sleep without the blanket. The small raft was crowded, with all five of them spread out to sleep, but he wanted to reserve their strength for when they landed. He wanted to get as far as possible as quickly as possible. With soldiers around…

He shut his eyes, willing himself to relax, for the sound of Ceianna's steering pole to lull him to sleep. And maybe, just maybe, for one of the dreams to come and tell him he was on the right track.

You found the riddle, he told himself. *You must be on the right track. That's probably why the dreams are absent.*

He clenched his hand into a fist, pulling the blanket tighter around him.

Eventually he began to drift off. The sounds of Ceianna guiding the boat, even the sense of her moving about the sleepers faded to a blur.

Then there was a rapid series of soft thuds, a splash, and something landed just an inch from his head. Another something flew over him, landing with a thump.

Chris threw back his blanket and rolled away enough to jump to his feet.

Ceianna stood, arms wrapped around Terrin's waist, attempting to pull the taller girl away from the edge of the raft. Terrin strained forward, her eyes wide and her face pale.

He stepped forward, blocking her way with his arm.

"Terrin, wake up. It's just a dream."

Her face turned slightly towards his. Her eyes were blank except for the panic. Her mouth was open, and her breath came in ragged gasps. A bead of sweat rolled down the side of her face.

"Terrin?" he said.

She blinked, and her straining lessened. Across the raft, Nora threw back her blanket and sat up, watching.

"It's just a dream, Terrin. Wake up. Please."

"Chris?" Terrin said softly.

Ceianna released her, and she slumped forward onto Chris's arm. Ceianna stepped back, and Chris lowered himself and Terrin to a sitting position.

"What happened?" said Terrin.

Chris glanced up at Ceianna. She shrugged and turned away.

"You got up a couple minutes ago," she said, "and wandered around for a bit. Next thing I know, you're running across the boat. We nearly didn't catch you."

"Shouldn't someone be steering the boat?" Terrin asked, glancing ahead.

"Looking for my— Ah!" Ceianna's hand flashed out and grasped a long rod sticking up from the water. Chris hadn't even noticed it in the poor light. With a sucking sound, Ceianna pulled her steering paddle free from the water and mud.

She threaded her way back to the head of the boat, and as she passed Terrin, she said, "I'm more interested in WHY you tried to take a swim."

Chris locked his gaze with Terrin's.

"You've been having the dreams, haven't you?"

"Of course, I've been having dreams. Everyone has dreams," she said, standing up and turning away.

"You know what I mean, Terrin. The type of dreams… like the one that made me ne—"

Terrin turned back towards him sharply, cutting him off with a wave of her hand.

"Terrin?" said Nora softly.

Terrin glanced at Nora, then collected her hair, pulling it back over her shoulders.

"Alright, maybe I have."

"That's how you found me and Thomas, isn't it?" Chris smiled as he made the connection.

Shrugging, Terrin sat back down. Nora came over and joined them.

Chris glanced at Ceianna. Her focus seemed locked on steering the boat, but she stood unnaturally still at the same time.

"So," he said, turning his attention back to Terrin, "you've been having the dreams."

The feeling of relief made him almost giddy.

"But what were you dreaming about, just now?" said Nora. Her eyebrows were knitting together.

"It's not important," Terrin said, tilting her head back.

"Of course it is," said Chris. "These dreams have already proved important."

"Well…" said Terrin, but she paused. Her gaze fell to her

hands, folded in her lap.

"Terrin, why wouldn't you tell us?" asked Nora.

"Fine," snapped Terrin. "In my dream, I woke up in a clearing. And there was some crazy old lady and a wraith. The woman kept going on about me being a fool to come into the swamp, and that I was a threat, and— She wanted me to do something. Then I ran away, which is when you woke me up."

They fell into silence. Arnold let out a loud snore, then rolled over.

"Well, at least someone is getting sleep," said Terrin.

Chris refused to be distracted.

"Terrin, what was it the woman wanted you to do? And where were you in the dream, exactly?"

She held his gaze for a minute, then dropped her eyes back to her hands. Her fingers tugged at the edge of her left sleeve.

"We were in a clearing in a forest. I think Xell, but I couldn't be sure. I don't know. She just wanted me to do something."

Chris considered pressing the issue, but discarded that idea.

"We should go back to sleep," he said. "Tomorrow will be a long day, no doubt."

As Chris knelt back down by his blanket, a thought crossed his mind. He looked over his shoulder to where the two girls were settling into their own beds.

"If you have any more dreams—if either of you have any more dreams—please, tell me. And also, Terrin, don't worry too much about the dream. I promise that we'll be there. We might not be able to stop the dream from happening, but I promise we won't let that woman hurt you."

Terrin looked over to him and opened her mouth, but snapped it shut again and turned back to her blanket.

Chris did not sleep much more that night.

$$\text{❧ 40 ❧}$$

Nora

"Nora, we're nearly there," said Terrin.

Nora drowsily opened her eyes. A pale hint of dawn glowed along the horizon—not a rosy dawn but gray, as though even the sky was covered in mud. She could barely see Chris at the head of the raft, talking with Ceianna. She rose, pushing back her blankets, while Terrin moved on to wake the others. Nora popped her neck, watching Terrin prod Arnold, who seemed to be clinging to sleep with all his strength.

Terrin acted like she'd forgotten her near soaking. Before, she had seemed shaken, but now she moved with her normal smooth and controlled motions. There were also no hints of tiredness on her face, which made Nora feel a bit jealous. She herself had struggled to get to sleep, even more so after the incident.

Nora turned and rolled up her blanket, and then rechecked her pack. By the time she was done, Chris had turned to face them.

"Ceianna says we have half an hour to an hour before we'll have to leave the boat. I'm hoping we can reach the horses by two, maybe three, this afternoon. But we need to know where we're going after that. So now, it's time to think about the riddle."

He sat down and ran his fingers through his hair, but they didn't get far before they were stopped by a knot. The others stopped working on their packs, and the five of them created a cross-legged circle.

"May I hear the riddle?" asked Ceianna, glancing back from where she remained at the front of the boat.

"Yeah, I should probably repeat it anyway," said Chris.

> "Air rushing, rushing by,
> Faster, faster than the eye.
> Far above the deep, deep blue,
> Where water dashes at the rocks.
> And higher still the great one flies,
> Guarding hope as watchmen pose."

When he finished, he looked around the circle, meeting everyone's eyes for a moment. "Ideas?"

"Well," said Arnold. "This may be a stretch, but I think it might be a windy place."

"Wow, Arnold," Terrin said. "That was so insightful. I don't know where these flashes of inspiration come from."

"My mother's side," he said, grinning.

"I think," said Thomas, "that it is also safe to assume it is next to the ocean…"

His voice trailed off as he grabbed his bag and pulled out a sheaf of papers. He selected one and spread it out on the boat, facing Chris.

"North Raec," Nora said, recognizing the map upside down.

"Yes, this is my map of North Raec. One of the finest, if I say so myself," said Thomas, smiling. "And here are the oceanside cliffs," he added, tapping a few spots on the map.

Nora attempted to read the names of the cliffs, but they were written in a swirly but cramped text that she couldn't read upside down in the scant light.

"Well, it sounds like there are a lot of rocks. But then, that's true for most cliffs, isn't it?" said Chris.

"Leastways, far as I know," said Thomas. "Which leaves the great one and the watchmen."

"Maybe the great one is a dragon," said Arnold, grinning. "They're pretty great."

"They're also pretty mythical," said Terrin, rolling her eyes.

"You know," Arnold said, "if you roll your eyes too much, they'll stay that way."

"That's when you cross your eyes."

"Oh," said Arnold, stretching the word out for a few seconds.

"If we could take this seriously for a moment," snapped Chris.

Nora looked up at him. There wasn't even a hint of smile in his face. She noticed, now, the shadows under his eyes. The beard that had been growing since they entered the swamp added to his exhausted look. And she had thought *she* wasn't getting much sleep.

"Well, the great one seems fairly obvious," said Ceianna. "Eagles are commonly considered the grandest of birds."

"Right. That makes sense," said Terrin. "Are any of the cliffs known for eagles?"

Thomas shrugged. "I don't know."

"Which leaves the watchmen," said Chris, rubbing his eyes.

"I think I actually *can* help with that," said Arnold, looking up. He pointed to some cliffs on the east side of North Raec, towards the south. "Here, Dawncliff. I don't know much about eagles, but Dawncliff is known for the many boulders there which, at least in some people's eyes, look like men gazing out across the ocean.

I suppose they could be considered watchmen."

"Well then," said Chris, a smile tugging at the corners of his mouth, "to Dawncliff it is."

❧ 41 ❧

Christopher

Two armed guards stood by the paddock where Marc and the other horses were grazing. Chris and his friends watched them from the shelter of the trees.

"Okay, so our welcome here might be gone," he whispered.

He fought the urge to curse. When he had heard there were soldiers in the swamp, Chris had hoped that their mission was related to the possible war Arnold had mentioned. But regardless of their original intent, this made it almost certain that his presence in North Raec was known.

"Ceianna, you should go back," he added. "You've done your job and more. And who knows how long we'll be waiting here for an opportunity."

Ceianna had insisted on accompanying them until they retrieved their horses. Despite not having slept in over twenty-four hours, she did not seem tired.

"I—" started Ceianna, but she was cut off by a sharp "shh" from Terrin.

Chris turned his attention back to the guards.

"How much longer you figure we have to wait?" said the first one, stroking Minty. "Nice horses they got."

"What is it with you and horses?" snapped the second. He leaned against the stable wall, his arms crossed. "And they could be back any time."

"Nah," said the first one. "The captain hasn't come back yet, so we should have a while."

"The captain was supposed ta be back yesterday. What if he got held up? What if one of them crazy swampers killed him?"

Chris glanced over to Ceianna. Her muscles had tightened, and her brow was creased. While the swamp people were generally considered crazy by the plainsmen, to call them so to their face was bordering on suicidal—depending on the people involved.

"You worry too much," said the first one. He gave Minty a final pat and turned to Marc. "They're just a bunch of kids, and it's not like—"

"What are you bedlams doing outside?" shouted a third man, bursting from the forest several yards to Chris's right. "Inside now. Go, go! What type of ambush is this? Bah!"

"Watch it, Cap," said the first guard. "Your accent is showing. And if they're close enough to see us standing about, they're more than close enough to hear you yelling your head off."

"And also," said the second one, bouncing off the wall, "if you'd come on time like you were supposed ta, we would be exactly where we were supposed ta be, exactly when we were supposed ta be."

"What's important right now is that I lost track of them, and they could be here any minute. So if you're not in position in three seconds, you'll be cleaning dishes and peeling potatoes for the rest of your army life!"

This time, Chris noticed the Diamond Isles accent the man was struggling to conceal. He filed that information away for further consideration.

Scowling, the two soldiers scurried to their hiding places, followed by their captain.

Chris turned to the others. "Okay, we need to make a plan. Preferably one that doesn't involve anyone getting hurt."

"I say go for the old distract-and-grab tactic," said Arnold.

"My thoughts exactly," said Chris, nodding. "Terrin and I are the best runners, so we'll distract the soldiers and draw them away. Arnold will stand guard, in case any of them return, while Nora and Thomas saddle the horses. When the two of us get back, we'll mount up and clear out as fast as we can."

"I'll help distract them," said Ceianna. "I'll be able to lose them just by looping back to the swamp."

"You needn't," said Chris. "Guiding us out of the swamp was plenty of help, and if you do this you could get in trouble. Your people could get in trouble."

"You have promised our people your friendship, and so we return it. I, even more so, since you would have risked your lives to save mine. I will help you retrieve your horses, to repay the debt, and there is nothing you can do to stop me."

Her eyes met his, and they flashed with determination.

"Fine," said Chris. He didn't have time to argue. "We'll fall back and eat lunch. Give them an hour or so to get bored, and then—"

"And then finalize our plans on a full stomach," cut in Thomas.

Chris smiled slightly and nodded.

❧ 42 ❧

Christopher

"You get the horses ready. I'll let the stable-master know we're back," said Chris, strolling into the clearing, struggling to keep his voice even.

"Okay," said Terrin, jogging past him to the stable. The horses looked up at their voices and greeted them with a chorus of whinnies.

"Hey, guys," Terrin said, pausing to pat Leaf before she turned towards the tack shed.

Chris's breath caught in his throat, but he forced himself to continue walking across the yard. If the soldiers were going to attack, they would do it soon, probably once Terrin picked up the saddle.

Then there was a loud yelp from one of the guards, and Terrin sprinted out of the stable yelling, "Run, run! Everyone run!"

One of the guards ran out of the stable right behind her.

Chris took up her shouts, waving his arms around. A second man emerged from the stable, glancing around. For a second, his and Chris's eyes met. It was the third guard—the captain.

Chris took off running.

He resisted the urge to look back and see if the man was following either him or Terrin. If he didn't, it would be Ceianna's job to try and draw him away.

And if that didn't work…

Well, Chris really hoped it would.

At first, Chris ran slowly, almost jogging. Then he heard someone crashing through the woods behind him and one glance over his shoulder gave him an extra burst of speed. The third guard was following behind him by only a couple yards.

As he ran, he searched the forest for signs of Terrin. There she was, ten yards or so off to his left. She wasn't running full out, for fear of leaving her guard behind. Chris glanced back and forth between the path ahead of him and Terrin. He didn't want to get too close to her. Whenever she made a turn, he responded to keep the distance.

Several times, his pursuer almost caught him, and he would have to throw on a special burst of speed to add distance. At some point, he lost track of Terrin and her pursuer. After what felt like an hour, though he was sure it couldn't have been much more than five minutes, the guard began to lag behind.

Suddenly Ceianna was beside him, pushing him to his right.

"Wraith pack… headed… this way," she said between breaths.

"Does Terrin know?" Chris said, stretching his legs to full speed.

Ceianna didn't answer, and Chris was running too hard to ask again.

Behind them, he heard a short scream. Chris glanced back in time to see a wraith standing over Chris's pursuer, glaring at one of the other guards. The men hadn't noticed a second wraith in the shadows. Chris slowed down to shout a warning, but Ceianna jerked him into a sharp turn that made him focus on where they were going. Ten minutes later, they stopped in a clearing.

"What about Terrin?" gasped out Chris, staring at Ceianna.

"I don't know," she spat out through her teeth. "I couldn't find her."

She was doubled up a bit, hands against her knees.

"How did you know they were coming?"

She hesitated. "I saw them."

"Saw them? I didn't notice anything."

"You weren't looking for them."

"And you were? Why?"

"Because… because…"

Chris strode across and grabbed her shoulders.

"Tell me," he hissed. "My friend is out there, and I need to find her. And if you know anything about it—"

"My grandmother kidnapped her," Ceianna said it with a huff, glaring at him with a force that made him step back.

"Why?"

She squeezed her head between her hands, as if she was resisting the urge to tear out her hair.

"Because she thinks that Terrin's going to raise an army and lead the forest people to war on the swamp people. And the swamp people couldn't withstand that. So she's decided to stop it."

Chris frowned.

"Why would she think that?"

"Because Terrin's a spirit-friend."

She said it as if it explained everything, but it confused Chris more.

"But Terrin hates spirits!" he said. "They scare her to death. She'd never be friends with them."

"Well, she is. Or at least she has the capability to be. And that makes her as dangerous as a wild dragon, as far as my gran's concerned."

Chris thought this over for a moment.

"And you agree with this?"

"I don't know," she snapped.

There was a short silence. Then she continued. "I think that it's wrong to kill her. Especially like this."

"Then will you help me rescue her?"

Ceianna nodded. "It was given to me to protect you. All of you, including her. And I'll do it."

"Good. Then find her and your grandmother. I'm going back to get the others. We'll meet back here."

Chris glanced up at the sky. Terrin had said that it had been around midafternoon in her dream. They didn't have much time.

∽ 43 ∽

Terrin

Terrin bent over a leather bag, which was spread flat across her lap. One hand held the bag steady, and in the other, she held a fine-tipped brush. She nibbled the inside of her left cheek as she lowered the brush, adding smooth, grayish-brown strokes to the other colors on the bag.

Another dream. The thought faded as soon as she had it. She tried to grasp it, but quickly found she couldn't focus on anything except her painting.

"Watcha workin' on, Roz?"

Someone plopped down beside her. Terrin looked—no, Roz looked around and saw the stocky youth craning his neck to see the bag.

Roz's cheeks grew warm.

"Oh, ah, nothing. Well, I mean, ah, you weren't—"

She glanced back down at the bag.

"Spit it out, Roz," said the tall, blond man. He sat down on Roz's other side.

"Well, I thought the bag Peter gave me looked a bit bland—I mean it's wonderful, but... so I decided to document our journey on it. Leaving out the harpies' cave, of course."

Roz held up the bag, careful not to smudge the paint.

Terrin examined her work. So far, there were three blocks of color, each about a hand-width square, and the beginning of a fourth, with small gaps between them. In the first picture, three riders drew near some mountains, above which harpies circled. In the second, they stood in a great cavern with green mist, and below them was another room with a stream running through it. A hump of stone with little black scratches on it sat beside the stream. Around the edges of the third picture, Roz had painted the letters N, W, E, and S in a swirling script. Between them stood a forest, shaped like an arrow and pointing downward to the S. From the gray brown color, Terrin knew that the swamp came next.

"Looks nice," said the blond man.

"Nice?" said the other. "It's her best work! I'm honored my bag has received such favor."

"Though," started the man, "shouldn't you wait till after the journey to paint it? I mean, besides being able to work on it at a proper table with proper light, there's also spacing. What if you end up with too much left over, or not enough room to finish?"

"Oh, uh..." once again Roz's gaze dropped. Then she smiled and said, "I wanted to work while the details were still fresh in my mind."

The man frowned. His eyes searched her face.

"Roselyn?" he said softly.

"Honestly, Miles, you shouldn't look at your sister like that," said Peter. "Though, you should take note, Roz, that you are far more beautiful than you portray yourself there."

Roz giggled.

"Yeah," said Miles, "and Peter should be fatter."

"Hey!" said Peter, jumping to his feet.

"That's what you get for flirting with my sister," said Miles.

"How about you two go duke it out somewhere else, and let me finish up here," said Roz, smiling. "Or better yet, you could start fixing supper."

"Alright, alright," said Peter, walking off. "Supper it is."

Miles also stood and started away. Then he paused and glanced back at Roz for a moment.

"We are going to make it, you know. All of us."

Then he turned and left.

❧

Terrin's eyes flickered open. Her cheek was pressed against soft blades of green grass. The world before her was slightly blurry. She sat up, blinking the daze away, and the world sharpened. She was in a clearing.

Familiarity washed over her. She leaped to her feet and spun to face the wraith that crouched behind her, just like it had in her dream. Which meant…

"So, you're finally awake," said a drawling voice.

Terrin turned, already knowing what she would see. An old woman—the one who'd been watching her for the past month—leaned against a tree.

"You were a fool, gallivanting around the swamp like that. That, more than anything, made me sure it was time to dispose of you, spirit-friend."

The woman spat at Terrin's feet, but Terrin jumped away.

"I don't know what you're talking about," Terrin said.

She wondered vaguely if she could change the dream. She

opened her mouth to say something else, but the woman cut her off.

"Lies!"

The woman's shout startled Terrin, and she burst into a run. Once she started, she didn't stop, leaping over a bush and out of the clearing. She heard the roar of the wraith behind her, and the woman shouted, "I know what you are, and you cannot hide it. Nor can you escape me!"

Terrin cut a sharp right to avoid a tree, and then she was past where the dream had ended. But this time, she wasn't pulled away from the world. This time she kept running.

This time it was real.

The underbrush caught at her legs, but she pushed through, swerving through the trees. She could hear the steady thumps of the wraith following her. She rounded another tree. Two wraiths stood in front of her, their teeth bared. She dove to the right, rolling and springing back to her feet, and ran again. She glanced over her shoulder to see the first wraith jump over one of the two, and then they all turned to follow her.

She looked forward again, putting all her energy into a burst of speed. She curved around another tree, but had to pull up short as a fourth wraith blocked her way. She turned left, but another one was already cutting her off that direction.

She spun, searching for an escape, but the wraiths had surrounded her and were circling closer and closer. They stopped a couple yards away, their eyes pinned on her.

The woman arrived a few minutes later.

"I see my pets have rounded you up," she said, her eyes glittering.

The four wraiths backed up, making room for the woman.

"Let me go," said Terrin. "I've done no harm to you or your

people, and I certainly don't intend to."

"Oh, don't worry. I am not a cold-blooded murderer. But I cannot allow a threat against my people to stand. So, I will give you a choice. If you call your spirit here, we will kill it and spare you. Otherwise…"

The woman's voice trailed off and her eyes locked with Terrin's.

"You know the truce as well as I do," Terrin snapped. "You can't kill me, nor would I ever harm your people."

The woman laughed.

"Ah, but the wraiths have been acting up lately, haven't they? There would be no proof of my involvement. Besides, even if I convinced my darlings to let you go today, the forest would never again be safe for you. So, call your spirit."

"I don't have a spirit, and I certainly can't call it. And even if I could, you can't kill a spirit. Your weapon would go right through."

"Ah, there you are mistaken," said the woman.

She drew out a dagger, nearly identical to Ceianna's.

"See, wraith teeth have the ability to tear apart spirit magic." She slid her hand along the white blade. "How else do you think we managed to fight you?"

"Okay, now I really don't have a clue what you're talking about," said Terrin, backing away. "If you wanna kill spirits go ahead, I won't stop you. But I can't call a spirit here. So let me go."

Her spine prickled.

She was alone.

Chris had said he'd be here, but even if he were, what could he do?

She was going to die.

The madwoman cursed. "You can't trick me, spirit friend. But if that is what you wish, no one can say that I didn't give you a chance."

The wraith nearest Terrin lunged. The prickling in her spine vanished, replaced by a feeling of absolute calm. The world seemed to have slowed down, particularly the wraith. It almost floated through the air.

Run.

The one, simple word flashed through her mind. She didn't need more prompting. She dove forward, under the wraith, then jumped back to her feet. The other three beasts charged, as the first landed with a howl. She sprinted forward, straight to the nearest tree, her eyes slid half shut. She didn't bother to even try jumping for the branch above her or looking for hand holds. She just ran, placing one foot then the next against the bark, pushing herself up. Running up the tree.

She felt her feet start to slip and forced herself to take one more step, then flung out her hand, catching the branch. She swung her body sideways, arcing her legs up and around. Her foot caught the branch. She hauled herself up, almost slipped, and pulled herself to her feet.

For a second, as she stood, pride fill her chest, and she wished that her brother could have seen.

Then a wraith lunged upward towards her, banishing the feeling. She turned and fled further up the tree. She didn't even pause to think about finding handholds, just climbed on instinct. She got up several feet, then leaped to the next tree.

"Follow her!"

Terrin glanced back and saw that the woman now rode one of the wraiths, which stood at its full height. The others were below the tree, golden eyes locked on Terrin.

Terrin ran.

$\mathcal{C}3$ 44 $\mathcal{C}3$

Arnold

"That way. We're almost there," whispered Ceianna, pointing off slightly to the left. "Just through those trees."

Arnold gave a short nod and held up his ha—stump to signal the others to stop as he reigned in Rich.

"Get off now," he said. "If there's a fight, I don't want you to fall off Rich."

"Of course," she said, relief obvious in her voice.

She quickly slipped off and put nearly two yards between her and the horse. Rich exhaled loudly, his muscles relaxing. Arnold couldn't help agreeing with the sentiment. Ceianna had been as tense as a scrunched spring—Arnold was pretty sure he'd have bruises in the morning from her crushing grip around his waist.

"If Terrin's not here," he said, meeting Ceianna's eyes.

All signs of her recent anxiety were gone, and once again her eyes were like stone. "As I told Chris, this is where my grand-mother would have brought her," she said.

Arnold nodded, wrapped his reins loosely about his saddle's

pommel, and drew his sword. As he did so, Chris passed him, and urged Marc into a fast trot towards the trees Ceianna had indicated. Arnold signaled with his legs for Rich to follow. Behind him rode Thomas on his horse, and then Nora on Minty, leading Terrin's horse Leaf.

Arnold was enveloped with the warmth of the afternoon sunlight as he rode into the clearing and stopped beside Chris, sword raised, ready for anything.

The clearing was empty.

Arnold looked expectantly to Chris, but his friend was silent, his back rigid.

℃

Christopher

"Ceian—" Arnold began to say, but Chris cut him off.

"No, this isn't her fault," he said. "Terrin was here, but she left, trying to escape. We're too late."

Chris shut his eyes. How would they find her now? What if they couldn't? Terrin had only told him the gist of her dream, but now he needed details.

Which way had she run?

"Terrin!" shouted Arnold.

Chris's eyes jerked open, and his attention turned to Arnold. The knight had let his sword droop, but his face was livid as he opened his mouth to shout again.

"Wait," said Chris.

"Do you have a better plan?" Arnold snapped.

Chris thought for a moment, then nodded. He turned Marc to face Ceianna, who stood just outside the clearing. Her head was bowed and her hands curled into fists.

"Ceianna, how good are you at tracking?"

She raised her head, and smiled slightly. "Poor, but I have a friend who will be able to find Terrin in a jiffy. He should be near here."

Chris raised an eyebrow, but instead of questioning her, said, "Go find him, then."

She turned and disappeared into the forest.

"Chris, can't you track?" asked Arnold. Beneath him, Rich pawed the ground.

"Barely," said Chris. "The forest here is thick, and I'd lose the trail pretty fast. I know you're impatient to find Terrin, but trust me. This will be quick—"

"Look!" gasped Nora, dropping Minty's reins to point up into the trees. Her other hand held Leaf's lead rope, and at the end of it, Leaf was nodding her head and whickering.

Chris turned to look, and his jaw dropped, then he smiled. Moving through the tree branches, as if she'd been born there, was Terrin. She reached the edge of the clearing and stopped, beaming down at them.

"You came!" she said.

Then, beneath her, a wraith burst into the clearing, followed by two more. The beasts glanced at Chris, and while one of them snarled, they stayed under Terrin's tree.

Then another wraith entered the clearing at full height, and on its back rode an old swamp woman.

45

Arnold

Arnold's joy at seeing Terrin quickly vanished.

The woman glowered at them and hissed. "I haven't time for you."

"Let Terrin go with us in peace. We don't want a fight," Chris said.

The woman shook her head, and her wraith pawed the ground. The other three beasts glanced at their leader, but quickly returned to watching Terrin.

"I'm afraid I can't let her go yet. She's helping me with a project."

"We aren't exactly in the mood for waiting. We are under the protection of the swamp. All of us—including Terrin. Therefore, you are bound to leave us be, for you are of the swamp."

She laughed, a high loud laugh that made Arnold's spine crawl. He tightened his grip on his sword and raised it.

"You," said the woman, her nose wrinkled with disdain, "are not in the swamp. Besides, she is of the forest, and the swamp holds no protection for the likes of her."

Arnold's patience snapped. Gripping the horse between his knees, he heeled Rich, and they leaped forward. The wraith twisted away as he charged past, forcing the woman to clutch at its scaly back.

Rich pivoted easily, tossing his head, ready for another dash.

The woman waved a hand, and two of the other three wraiths turned away from Terrin to face Chris and Arnold.

Chris drew his sword, and Marc charged their wraith.

Then Arnold's wraith sprung. Rich danced out of the way so that Arnold could take a glancing blow at the wraith's legs. As the creature landed, it spun to face them. Again it dashed by Rich, clawing at the horse as it passed. Rich squealed, lowering his head as he narrowly avoided the wraith's attack. Arnold signaled Rich with just the touch of his heel, and the horse pivoted to face the wraith.

Arnold's mouth was a grim line. He was a bit worried at what these wraiths were capable of, but he knew Rich could handle it.

The wraith straightened its legs, arching its back as it raised to almost Rich's height. It snapped at Arnold, showing its white teeth and pink tongue. Then it lunged. Rich sidestepped away, turned to face the wraith and reared. Arnold's knees tightened on the horse and he leaned forward, wrapping his left arm around the pommel. Beneath him, Rich's hooves thrashed against the wraith.

The wraith screeched and fell back. As Rich came back to four legs, Arnold straightened and followed up his advantage. Steering Rich to the wraith's side, he struck down at it repeatedly. The monster dropped back low to the ground, but Arnold leaned down to jab at it a few more times.

A horn blew loudly.

Arnold lifted his head for a second to see what had happened, letting the wraith escape from his attack.

Three men rode into the clearing—the ones from before, the Diamond Isles captain and two soldiers. All three had swords drawn, but they looked more concerned about the wraiths than the fugitives they'd no doubt come here after.

With a quick glance, Arnold took in the rest of the clearing. Nora was still at the edge of the woods, holding Leaf and looking for a way to reach Terrin, who was still guarded by the third wraith. Thomas was in battle with the old woman, who used a knife much like Ceianna's.

Arnold turned his head back too late. The wraith had only fled for a second, then spun with lightning speed, lunging and bowling Rich over. Arnold managed to kick his feet free from the stirrups and push himself just clear of the falling horse.

Rich surged back to his feet, knocking the wraith aside and then chasing after it, kicking as fiercely as he could.

Arnold knew he should move, get clear of Rich's flashing hooves. But he was stunned, partly by the fall, but also by the similarity to the scene a month earlier. He shut his eyes and could see the ginger wolf snarling at him. His left hand, or at least its ghost, throbbed.

Then he set his jaw, imagined his left hand clenching into a fist, and rolled to the side, slowly sitting up as he took several deep breaths. He scanned the clearing, forcing himself to focus.

Terrin was still in the tree, her whole body rigid as she watched the conflict. Nora was fighting one of the soldiers and having some trouble. Leaf had escaped her hold and now wandered on the edge of the battle, tossing her head and snorting, but not fleeing.

Chris seemed to be in a three-way dual with a wraith and the captain. Thomas was still in combat with the woman, while the third soldier was pitted against the remaining wraith—and losing.

Arnold got back to his feet, sheathed his sword, and whistled. Then he sprinted forward. Rich kicked the wraith one last time, good and hard, then cantered a few strides, slowing just as he reached Arnold. Arnold caught the pommel, set his toe in the front of the stirrup and pushed himself up, swinging over the horse. As he settled, he slid his toe from the stirrup and put it back in the right way. He turned Rich to face the wraith once more, and drew his sword again.

The beast gathered itself to its feet. One eye was tightly closed, and it had several cuts along its side. Still it attacked, lunging forward at Arnold and Rich. Arnold slashed upward, catching the inside of its leg with his sword. The wraith howled and fell, its tail lashing back. Rich reared again, striking at the fast-approaching tail, and Arnold held tight as his horse danced. When they came down again, he swung at the wraith's already wounded eye. It screamed again. After a last swipe with its claws, it bounded away, yowling.

Arnold looked around. The soldier who had been fighting a wraith alone was on the ground, his horse nowhere to be seen. The wraith towered over him. Arnold pushed Rich into a run. His sword struck uselessly at the wraith's neck as he went by, but it distracted the beast. It turned, and hissing loudly it launched itself at Arnold.

Arnold yelled for the man to escape, but instead he scrambled up and ran to Arnold's side. Together, they battled the wraith.

46

Nora

Minty swerved, but she was a bit too slow. The soldier's shining blade sliced across Nora's leg. She yelped, then gritted her teeth. Around the edges of her eyes a blue-gray fog began to spread, blocking her vision. She blinked rapidly, and it cleared. She mentally shook herself as she turned Minty to strike back at the soldier.

Chris's voice rose over the clanging and howling and hissing. "Retreat, fall back. Run. Flee."

Nora turned Minty and pushed her into a fast trot. She bent and grasped Leaf's lead-rope as she went by, wincing as pain jabbed through her leg. They made for Terrin's tree. Fortunately the swamp woman had fled on her wraith, and the way to Terrin was clear.

As they approached, Terrin dropped from the branches and bent to grab something from the ground. Then she took Leaf's lead and mounted. Leaf burst into a canter.

Nora clucked at Minty to follow. The horse bunched beneath

her, but then the soldier and his horse jumped in front of them. Minty skittered, turning sharply to avoid a collision. Nora clutched at the saddle with one hand to keep from being thrown. In the other hand, she held her sword away from her horse. The soldier raised his sword to strike while she still struggled not to fall.

Then a wraith at full height burst between them, snapping at the man. Ceianna was perched on its back. The swamp girl shouted for Nora to go.

Nora didn't have much choice. Minty had jumped away from the wraith and was all too glad to run like crazy. They raced past blurred trees and bushes, bounding over anything in her way. Air whipped through Nora's hair and tore her breath away. Hanging tightly to her horse's mane, Nora forgot about the sword, still gripped in her hand, until it nearly ran into an oak.

"Whoa!" she cried, catching the reins and sitting deeply in the saddle.

Minty slowed.

"Whoa!" Nora said again, and this time Minty came to a full stop.

Nora sighed with relief. Then she bent over to examine both herself and her horse. Minty panted heavily, her sides foamed with sweat. Nora's right leg was bleeding badly, and both of them had several nicks and cuts of varying sizes.

Nora steadied her breathing. She wiped off her blade on her clean pant leg before sheathing it. Then she looked around cautiously, listening hard.

Nothing.

She was alone.

She dismounted, staggering as her legs once again took her weight. She leaned against Minty, gathering her strength.

After a minute, she searched through her saddle bag and

pulled out her roll of bandages. It took some effort to bind her leg, her hands trembling.

Next she found her water bag and took a small sip.

It wasn't much, but it would have to do. Even if neither the soldiers nor the swamp woman was searching the woods for her and the others, Minty needed to be cooled off by a long walk before either of them could rest.

So, instead of collapsing into a small ball and sleeping, Nora took Minty's reins and started east at a limping walk.

Chris had given them instructions. If they were separated, head for River's Cross, a small village, barely a village at all, really. Just an inn and a couple of farm houses that sprouted up around a bridge. It was northeast from where they were now, which meant they had to go out of their way, but it was out of the way of everyone else, too. With only open country and a few farms to pass through, it was as safe a place as any for fugitives to meet up.

So, to River's Cross they would go.

ℝ

Arnold

"Ow!" Arnold yelped.

Thomas shook his head and continued to apply the weird gray mush to Arnold's many cuts.

Ceianna paced the clearing.

"There, done," Thomas said, standing. "And if you would have stopped complaining, it wouldn't have hurt so much. Now, for your horse."

"You should have tended Rich first."

Thomas tutted. "I'm not the type to consider an animal, of any quality, more important than a human being."

Arnold ignored the healer and walked over to Ceianna.

"Why are you still here?"

Ceianna glanced at him. She snapped her fingers and a wraith appeared from the shadows of some bushes. Her hand settled against its neck and rubbed the scales there. Though pleased by the attention, the wraith watched Arnold with narrowed eyes.

"I'm watching out for you," Ceianna said.

"We're out of the swamp's protection. And the longer you stay with us, the more danger you'll be in."

"I knew what my grandmother was going to do. I should have acted sooner, should have protected Terrin. I should have known that my grandmother was wrong about her." Ceianna sighed. "I knew it, but I didn't act on it. The elders will punish me."

"Hey, you did what was right in the end. And you probably saved Nora's life."

Arnold bit his lip at that thought. He was worried for the Yorc girl, for all his friends. He hadn't seen which way she or Chris or Terrin had gone, but he hoped the three of them were together.

Ceianna shrugged.

"So," said Arnold, tentatively reaching out one hand towards the wraith. "Is this the friend you were talking about, the one that was going to find Terrin?"

"Yes. I have cared for him since I was very young. In some ways, he is my closest friend. His name is Fish."

"Fish?" said Arnold, choking on a laugh.

The wraith, who had nearly let him touch it, jerked back his head.

"Terrin's horse is named Leaf," said Ceianna.

"True," said Arnold, and quickly changed the topic. "So, wraiths are good trackers?"

"Not really. Their natural prey is fish, which cannot be tracked.

But Terrin is tinged with spirit magic, which they sense easily."

"Spirit magic? Because she was attacked by a spirit once?"

Ceianna looked up from the wraith and met Arnold's eyes.

"Attacked by a spirit?" she said, a smile tugging at the edge of her lips. "No spirit would ever attack any forest person, most certainly not Terrin."

"But—" Arnold paused. "What do you mean?"

"Terrin is a spirit-friend. That is why my grandmother fears her."

"Spirit-friend? I don't understand. Terrin hates spirits."

"That is what Christopher said. But—"

This time Ceianna paused, thinking.

"Long ago," Ceianna finally said, "the swamp people and the forest people were at war. Each had their own allies. The swamp people had the wraiths, which we rode into battle, and the forest people had spirits. Working together, a forest person and a spirit were very powerful, for spirits are a part of the forest, and through them the forest people could shape the forest. It was a potent bond, as strong as mine to Fish. Perhaps stronger in its own way.

"But when the plains people came and we chose one of them to lead both our people, they insisted that we put aside our differences. But the only peace we could come to, was if both our peoples would break our bonds. So the spirits isolated themselves in the Dark Forest, and no longer do the swamp people each select a wraith for their own. It was left to my family—my ancestor's family—to watch the wraiths and keep them from going wild."

Arnold's mouth was gaping long before she finished. And it took him some time to put any words together.

"That is some history," he finally managed.

She laughed. "I suppose so. The point is, though, that Terrin is a spirit-friend, the first for hundreds of years. For whatever reason, a spirit broke the treaty and bonded with her. Whatever her feelings towards the spirits are, that is the truth. My grandmother fears her for it, fears that she will attempt to destroy what remains of the swamp people."

"She would never!"

"I know. But the fact remains that the spirits have broken the treaty."

Arnold's hand curled to a fist as he tried to take it all in.

"You're right, though," said Ceianna. "I should go. My grandmother will be angry, and I'd like to be back in the city by the time she recovers."

"Won't she go there?"

"No. She knows that they won't support her actions. The wraiths are tending her now. She won't return until she's healed."

She hesitated, concern in her eyes. "Will you be able to find your friends?"

"Yes. We'll head to River's Cross as planned. We'll find each other there."

Ceianna nodded.

"I hope you do. I wish you luck. Here." She pulled from her travel bag a leather pouch and handed it to him.

He opened it as neatly as he could with one hand. Inside were many leaves, each with one yellow side and one vibrant green, their edges sawed.

"I wish I could give you a better gift. But this is all I have time for. Swamp people use it to purify and sweeten our water. However—" Here she paused and her eyes met Arnold's, and he saw a glint of amusement there. "Some people say it helps with ghost itches as well, but," she shrugged, "who can tell?"

⌘

Chris

"I'm sorry Terrin. I shouldn't have let you get captured like that."

He rode side by side with his forest friend at a trot, making for the rendezvous as planned. He was scratched up pretty bad, and a long cut over his forehead hurt like crazy, but none of the cuts seemed deep, and Terrin wasn't hurt at all.

She shook her head.

"No, we both knew it would happen. Just like the dream said."

Chris glanced at her and his brow furrowed. Knowing how she felt about magic, and how she liked to be in control, he was sure that having her life predicted by magical dreams must irk her to no end.

"But," she said with a smile, "you kept your promise. You came for me, just as fast as you could."

Chris shrugged. "Not fast enough. I should have been right on your tail."

Terrin sighed and looked up through the tree tops.

"There you go, acting like we're your charges or something. I ran distraction, knowing what might happen. I knew that you might not be there. There was a point when I really thought you wouldn't. But you came."

"And I always will."

"No, you won't," she snapped. "And you know it."

He bowed his head. She was right. He was very much afraid of the day when he wouldn't be there to help his friends. That was why he had left them, a little over a month ago. Tried to leave them behind.

But leaving them behind wasn't an option. He needed their help to finish this quest.

"And we know it, too," Terrin added. "But it doesn't matter, because you need us just as much, if not more, than we need you."

"You're right," said Chris, smiling. "Where would I be without you to keep my head on straight?"

"Very, very much turned around and lost," said Terrin matter-of-factly. Then she grinned.

"So," he said, "which way to River's Cross?"

"Now that you mention it, we are angled a bit south. Your fault, to be sure."

"Ah," said Chris, turning Marc northward. "There we go. On to River's Cross then."

❧

Terrin

As Chris turned his back to her, Terrin's smile faded. Her hand fell to the fox figurine on her belt. Her fingers closed around it, rubbing the smooth wood.

If the soldiers knew they were there, so would the king. Soon her family would know that it might be far more than a year before she returned. Her people would never go against the king. Her home was shut to her now.

She closed her eyes for a moment, holding back the pain. She was Terrin of Xell. She was on a mission to keep her friends safe. She didn't have time to be sad. She had to keep moving forward.

Terrin's eyes opened, and a smile spread across her face as she echoed Chris's words.

"On to River's Cross, then."

❦ 47 ❦

Brayden

As soon as Brayden and Gillian had returned from the castle, the ambassador had begun lecturing. It hadn't helped when partway through, the prince had remembered the letter from Gillian's father. Gillian read it in a pensive silence, and after that he railed on Brayden even more zealously—all about how he was sent only as a messenger, and what did he know about politics?

Words he would never have dared to say to Tyler.

With a huff, Brayden rolled over in his bed and squeezed his eyes shut, trying to sleep. Eventually he dozed, but he woke again at the slightest creak.

Giving up on sleep, he rolled to stare at the ceiling.

The curtains of the north-facing window rustled in a breeze that made him shiver. He would have shut the window, but then the room would be too stuffy, so instead he had worn his socks to bed. Now he pulled his blankets tighter.

There was another creak, closer this time. He sat up, staring towards the door.

It's probably nothing, just the house groaning, he told himself. Nonetheless, as he lay back down, he grabbed the dagger that rested on his bedside table and turned so he could still see the door. The clouds shifted. Reflected moonlight spread across the floor, lighting the handle just in time for him to see it start to turn.

He shut his eyes and forced himself to breathe deeply and evenly—both for the sake of feigning sleep, and in an attempt to steady his pounding heart. He gripped the edge of the blanket in his left hand.

He didn't hear the door swing open, but he heard the soft click when it shut.

He forced himself to wait the count of three. Then he tightened his grip around the knife and flicked the blanket to the side, springing from the bed.

He briefly registered a man standing a couple yards from the bed.

With another flick of his wrist, Brayden hurled the blanket at him. The man blocked the blanket and flung it aside with his sword arm, and as he did so, Brayden heard a small 'swish', and saw the glint of moonlight on metal.

He jumped backwards onto the bed, then dropped down on the other side, the thump of his landing muted by his socks. He dropped to a fighting position. The attacker followed, springing across the bed and landing in his own fighting stance. The man raised his blade, a wickedly curved knife, then fell on him with a flurry of blows.

Brayden deflected the man's blows with his own knife. He never thought he'd be grateful for those endless swordplay lessons.

Dodge, dodge.

Block, parry.

The man knew what he was doing. No sooner had the prince

survived one blow than he had to block the next.

Gritting his teeth a bit, Brayden darted to the side, hoping to slip around his attacker. But the man spun and pressed his attack, driving him toward the wall. The prince threw himself backward on the floor and felt a swish of air as the man's sword passed above him. He swept his leg up, kicking hard at the side of the man's knee. The man buckled and fell, but landed on his hands and started to roll away.

Brayden leaped to his feet and dove onto his opponent's back. He dug his knee into a kidney while he brought his knife to the man's throat.

He tried to keep from panting as he hissed through his teeth, "Who sent you?"

The man twisted himself sideways, his knife slicing at the prince's arm. Brayden jerked back, and his dagger slipped, sinking into the man's throat.

The man fell limp, and Brayden scrambled away, mouth hanging wide. A drop of sweat drizzled into his eye. He blinked it away, and then wiped his brow with his sleeve. Another breeze blew through the window, and he shivered.

I killed someone, Brayden thought, still gaping at the man.

Someone tried to kill me!

He pulled himself to his feet and staggered towards the door, still watching the body.

Then he stopped as a horrible, cold thought occurred to him. What if Gillian was involved? Or one of the servants?

No, the only reason for someone to kill him now would be to start a war. Gillian, though he perhaps wasn't trying too hard to stop the war, certainly didn't want it that bad.

Still, if he told Gillian, the ambassador was likely to lose his temper and start the war anyway. As long as there was a chance for peace, Brayden couldn't allow that.

He fell to his knees and covered his face with his hands.

Someone tried to kill him to start a war, and if anyone found out, the war would start anyway. So now he had a dead assassin on his floor, and he couldn't tell anyone.

Great. Just. Great.

ﳏ 48 ﳏ

Terrin

Terrin's eyes swept across the shadowed forest. She leaned against a tree, and the bark pressed into her shoulder.

Behind her, Chris and the horses slept. Chris had suggested traveling through the night, but she had vetoed the idea—only partly because it was foolish to lose sleep on the slim chance that someone had followed them.

She pushed off the tree and turned, looking in all directions. Then she glanced down at Chris. As far as she could tell, he was soundly asleep.

She went to her saddle pack and knelt. She didn't have to look hard to find the swamp woman's knife. Its white blade shone dully in the moonlight. The wooden handle was smooth, with two ridges for her fingers to rest against. She took it, and with one last glance over Chris and the horses, she stalked silently into the forest northward.

About twenty yards from camp, she stopped. A stiff breeze swept past her, and she shuddered. She held the knife loosely, its flat side pressed against her leg.

This is stupid. You don't know if the spirit will come.

And if it does, the knife might not work. You only have the word of one crazy lady.

Terrin shook her head, dismissing the doubts.

She needed to figure out how to make the spirit come. The first time she'd seen the spirit, she had been near its territory. And it had been there when she'd saved Chris and Thomas by the cliff. But now the Dark Forest was miles away.

Still, the spirit had come yesterday, so it must have been close by.

What would draw it to her?

She'd sensed spirit magic many times. Never when she wanted to, though.

The baby fox. The spirit had come that night, hadn't it? When she'd been trying to sooth the fox.

She shut her eyes and started to hum softly. Tuneless, at first. Her mind reached out, feeling for the tingling that signaled the spirit's approach.

Then of its own accord, a melody started to emerge. The melody grew—and with it, a tingle in her spine. Her eyes flew open. She stopped humming. Her eyes flickered to and fro, searching the woods for the ethereal glow. She did not have to look hard. In the darkness of night, it was easy to see the glimmer of the spirit through the trees. As it approached, Terrin could hear that it, too, was humming.

Soon she could see it clearly. Aside from the transparency and rose-colored hue, the spirit looked like a normal human woman. Its hair was thick and wavy, and it wore a long dress that trailed along the ground, passing more through the grass than over it.

Terrin had no idea how different one spirit might look from

another, but she felt sure that this was the first spirit, from her childhood.

Her heart thudded in her chest.

Still several yards off, the spirit stopped. She met its eyes, and the tingle ran sharply up her spine. Her breath caught in her throat, and for a moment she fought the urge to bolt, to flee the unnatural thing.

The spirit smiled. It held out one hand, palm up. Its humming grew louder.

Instinctively Terrin raised the dagger, holding it straight out. A beam of moonlight caught the white blade. The spirit flinched back, dropping its arm.

The hum stopped. The spirit turned to leave.

She lowered the knife and called, "Wait."

It paused and looked back over its shoulder.

She raised the knife again. "I—I want answers," she snapped.

It was a foolish request. After all, how could a spirit give her answers? It was a monster, even if it could talk—which she doubted—how could she trust anything it said?

The spirit hummed a quick, questioning hum, and met her eyes.

Terrin held its gaze, trying to hide her fear behind a stone face.

The spirit made a sound somewhere between a hum and a sigh. Then it hung its head, turned away again, and fled north.

And as it left, Terrin felt something cold settle in her chest. No—more than cold, it was empty.

Her gaze fell to the wraith-tooth knife, its blade still gleaming white in the watery moonlight, and the urge came to fling it as far away from her as she could, to wail like a child.

She shook herself.

That is a foolish thought, she chided.

But even as she returned to their camp and tucked the knife back in her bag, even hours later when she woke Chris for his turn at watch and laid down to sleep, the empty hole in her chest remained.

$\sim$

STILL NOT THE END

$\sim$

ABOUT THE AUTHOR

Homeschooled teen author Teresa Gaskins was creating stories before she could write. She enjoys a wide variety of fiction, fantasy has always been her favorite genre. She finished *Hunted* (her second published novel) when she was fifteen years old.

Teresa has recently picked up archery, shooting with a recurve bow much like Terrin's. Other interests include horse riding, computer programming, and making videos. She lives with her cat Cimorene (and the rest of her family) in rural Illinois, surrounded by corn and soybean fields.

If you would like to read more of Teresa's writing or send her a message, please visit her blog:

TeresaGaskins.com

DON'T MISS OUT!

Get Teresa's 50-page booklet of short stories and tips for young writers—and be one of the first to hear about her next book. Join the *Tabletop Academy Press Updates* email list on her blog or at the Tabletop Academy website:

TeresaGaskins.com
TabletopAcademy.net/Subscribe

CONTINUE THE ADVENTURE...

How can a knight fight magic?

Trained by the greatest knight in North Raec, Sir Arnold Fredrico dreamed of valiant deeds. Save the damsel. Serve the king.

Dreams change. Now the land teeters at the brink of war. As a fugitive with a price on his head, Arnold struggles to protect his friends.

But their enemy wields more power than the young knight can imagine.

If you love exploring fantasy worlds wracked by the struggle of good against evil, grab *Betrayed*—the third installment in Teresa Gaskins's four-book serial adventure, *The Riddled Stone*.

A gift she never wanted.
A curse she can't escape.

Alone in the dark, Nora of Yorc feels the dungeon walls pressing in. Even worse, the duke's sorcery weaves itself around her, unseen and deadly. But as the spell tightens, shy, fragile Nora breaks—and something new takes her place.

Or something old beyond memory.

Nora joined this quest to help her friends. But can she stop herself before the wildness within destroys them all?

If you love epic struggles of good against evil, don't miss *Revealed*, the exciting conclusion of Teresa Gaskins's four-book serial fantasy adventure, *The Riddled Stone*.

FOR ORDERING INFORMATION VISIT:
TABLETOPACADEMY.NET/FANTASY-FICTION